PUNISHED—A SCI-FI ALIEN WARRIOR ROMANCE

Raider Warlords of the Vandar #5

TANA STONE

Broadmoor Books

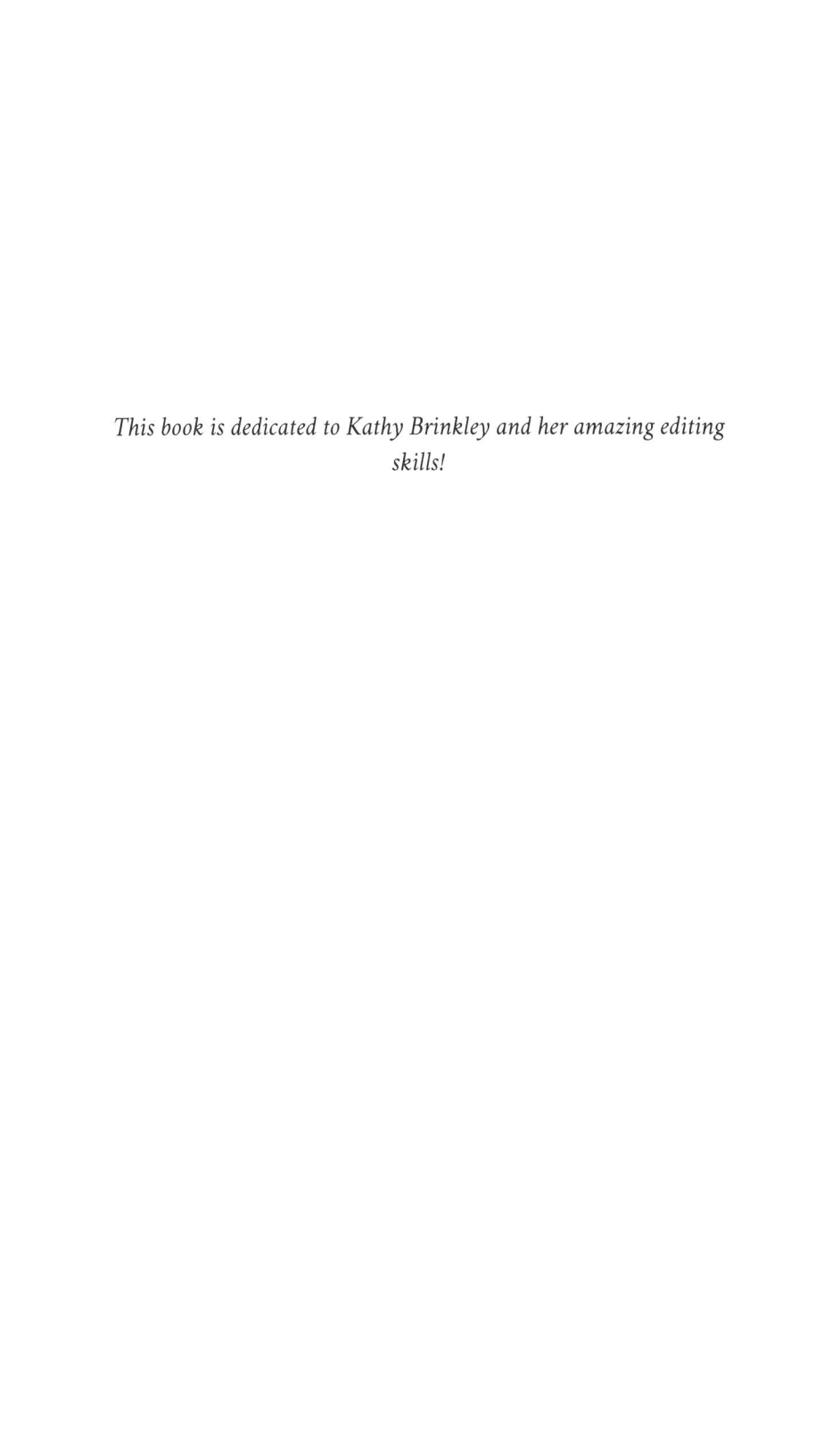

This book is dedicated to Kathy Brinkley and her amazing editing skills!

CHAPTER ONE

Corvak

"*Tvek,*" I muttered to myself as I stepped outside the door to my dwelling, bumping my head on the low doorframe and then straightening once I was beyond it. I inhaled the morning air that was already arid. Soon the two suns would be high in the sky and the heat would be intense, but for now it was bearable.

Curious faces that had been poking from windows and peering through cracks in doors popped inside once I appeared. I let out a low growl. As a Vandar raider, I was still a curiosity on the planet of Kimithion III. Not only was I the only Vandar on the planet, I was there because I'd been exiled by my horde. The Kimitherians and humans who populated the pre-warp planet had agreed to accept me into their community because the Vandar Raas I'd defied had rewarded them handsomely.

My exasperation at the curious Kimitherians morphed into a flush of humiliation as I thought of the series of actions that had landed me on the alien planet. I curled my hands into fists as I stomped down the narrow dirt pathway that wound around the stone mountains—dust kicking up around my boots—and passed the many dwellings cut into them. Curtains fluttered in triangular windows as I walked by quickly without looking right or left, even though the savory scents of breakfast foods wafted out and made my nose twitch.

Not long ago, I'd been the battle chief of a horde of the Vandar raiders, living and flying in a black-hulled warbird that moved invisibly through the galaxy. I'd led my fellow warriors into valiant battle against our enemy, the Zagrath Empire, our attacks punctuated by drinking and fucking on the occasional pleasure planet. It had been a life I'd relished, and a job at which I'd excelled. Nothing stoked my inner fire like a battle, whether with ships or with battle axes.

I rested my hand on the hilt of the circular battle axe that hung at my side. At least they had not taken that from me when they'd expelled me from the horde. My face heated as I thought back to having to trudge down the ramp of the warbird and set foot onto the alien planet. It had taken every bit of self-control I possessed not to rush back into the belly of the ship and beg for mercy. But I would never have shamed myself or the Raas by begging, even though I would have preferred to be executed than exiled. Raas Bron thought he was showing me mercy by exiling me instead of putting me out an airlock, but I would have much preferred a quick death in space than languishing on this alien wasteland.

I raised a hand to shield my eyes from the rising suns as they crested the sharp mountain spires that jutted into the air and encircled expansive turquoise shallows. Many would have considered the stark landscape beautiful, but to me it was only a reminder that I was not on a Vandar ship. The light that turned the sky violet was too bright for a warrior used to the shadows and iron of a horde ship. And for a Vandar warrior, there was nothing worse than not being on a raider ship.

"You have no one to blame but yourself," I said aloud, not caring if the locals who were watching me could hear or not.

It was true. Even though a part of me hated the Raas for dumping me on Kimithion III, another part of me knew I'd given him little choice. I'd defied the horde's warlord and then challenged him to a duel, which I'd lost. It didn't matter that I'd done it because I believed the horde to be in danger. I'd taken the human female that Raas Bron had claimed—a female I still believed was not who she said she was—and tried to extract the truth from her. She hadn't told me anything, and the Raas had been livid when he'd discovered what I'd done.

I did not regret my actions. I maintained that the female was a danger to the horde, and it was my duty as battle chief to protect the Vandar from all enemies. But I also understood why Bron could not allow my disloyalty to go unpunished. In a Vandar horde, the Raas ruled with ultimate power. Challenging that power and losing meant death. I accepted that. What I did not accept was the shame of exile.

I growled low and scraped a hand through my long hair as I reached the end of the steep path that brought me to the open square of the village. Wide paving stones were smeared with dust, and a central obelisk rose not much higher than my own head. The few shops and vendors circling the square—their doors and windows also cut into the stone of the mountain—were barely unshuttering their windows and propping open their doors.

Since arriving, I'd spent most of my time in the quarters I'd been assigned, but I'd noticed the village when I'd arrived since going through it was the only way to reach the cliffside residences. It reminded me of many primitive villages I'd seen before—quaint shops selling provisions ranging from food to clothing to tools, a cafe offering simple meals and drinks, and even a reading room stocked with books printed on nearly transparent sheets of seaweed. There was a free-standing school building for the village children—the only structure that appeared to be made from wood—and a cluster of open-air stalls for residents to see their wares. A few children played in front of the school with sticks and hoops, their laughter cutting through the quiet. It was all orderly and peaceful, with residents going about their business in apparent harmony. It made me want to hit something.

Why did my exile have to be *here*? Although they were not fully primitive, with running water and power along with basic technology to facilitate off-world trading and communication, the residents of Kimithion III did not possess ships capable of light speed or any significant weaponry. They engaged in limited trade with other planets, primarily because they had little of unique value to exchange. The land wasn't arable enough for large-scale farming, and their planet's core contained no valuable minerals. They did have rich waters from which they harvested sea creatures and water plants for food and medicinal purposes, but that wasn't something other planets valued as much as the planet's natives did.

From what I'd learned, they managed to do enough of a trade in kelp and seaweed powders to acquire the grains and other supplies they didn't produce, but residents didn't enjoy much in the way of luxury. Clothes were basic, personal ornamentation was not favored, and the dwellings cut into the cliff face were simply furnished. The flip side was that they held nothing of value to attract the empire's notice, which was why they'd been allowed to live without Zagrath interference. That, and they were a tiny planet, with only a few pockets of residents gathered around the planet's wide seas, which they called the shallows. The empire paid little attention to such an insignificant planet with nothing to mine for profit.

Which was one of the reasons why I was there, living in the largest of the planet's villages. No imperial soldiers to notice me or for me to attack. I grunted. At this point I'd be thrilled to see an imperial soldier to save me from the boredom of the rudimentary society.

The alien planet might not be a total wasteland, but compared to the sophisticated technology of the Vandar ships, it felt like living with barbarians. I understood the irony of that thought because since I'd arrived, most of the natives had been eyeing me like *I* was the barbarian. It probably didn't help that—like all Vandar raiders—I wore only a leather battle kilt and my boots with an occasional strap around my chest. Everyone else on the planet wore cloaks that covered them from head to toe or hooded jackets and long pants to protect them from the dust and heat.

A Kimitherian stepped from one of the shops, his iridescent, greenish-blue scales flashing at me from beneath his hooded cloak. He raised a webbed hand when he saw me, and I nodded in return, reminding myself that growling at everyone would not make my tenure on the planet any easier.

He ducked back into his shop, then returned moments later holding out a cup. When he crossed to me, he held it out. "Kimithion tea."

Even though he spoke the universal tongue, his words were staccato. I'd heard the native language, and it wasn't more than a series of sharp clicks that were nothing like Vandar or the universal tongue. He held out the cup without blinking, vertical pupils in his yellow eyes holding mine.

I considered waving him off, but I didn't want to be rude. After all, I was stuck here for the foreseeable future.

"Thank you." I took the cup and gave him a small bow of my head.

His wide, green lips stretched into his version of a smile as he watched me take a tentative sip and then freeze. "It is made with algae from the shallows." His grin became a chuckle as I choked on the pungent beverage. "It will make you live forever."

"I don't think it's the tea that does that," I said, as he turned and hurried back to his shop, his ivory cloak snapping around his bare, webbed feet.

Although the drink did taste of murky seawater, the warmth of the liquid filled my belly, so I finished it while I considered what he'd said.

His words had been in jest. The tea didn't make the people on the planet live forever—at least I didn't think it was the strange beverage—but, the fact was, the residents of Kimithion III *did* have unnaturally long life.

My first evening on the planet, I'd been visited by a representative from the Kimitherians and one from the humans. The two males had explained to me that the planet contained some sort of energy that granted its inhabitants lifespans that lasted hundreds of solar rotations. It wasn't that they were immortal. They could be killed by accident or violence, but they did not age noticeably once they reached maturity.

I swallowed the last tangy dregs of the tea, shaking my head both from the taste and the unbelievable story they'd told me. At first, I'd been skeptical, but they had no reason to lie to me.

Not only that, but their population also contained no aged residents, and I myself had experienced a strange phenomenon I couldn't explain away.

I raised a hand to my face, my fingers going instinctively to the scar that cut across my cheek. The one I'd gotten in a particularly bloody battle with the Zagrath. While it hadn't vanished, it had become thinner over the days. Now instead of a bumpy slash, it was a raised seam.

Taking long strides to the tables the Kimitherian was placing outside his shop door, I handed him back his earthenware cup. "Thank you for the tea. What do I owe you?"

The alien waved his hands, the heavy sleeves of his cloak flapping. "It is we who owe you for training our young males."

I almost groaned at the reminder. Another part of the visit from the community representatives had been their impassioned plea that I help them train a militia so they could defend themselves against the imperial incursion they were convinced was coming. Although the Zagrath were not yet aware of the incredible property of the planet, as soon as they were, the planet was in danger. Living forever was something the empire couldn't resist, and something they wouldn't allow the primitive Kimitherians and humans to possess. The people of the planet would find themselves removed and dumped onto another planet while the Zagrath built up Kimithion III for their own people and solidified their power over the galaxy as immortals.

I gritted my teeth. It was something I would never allow to happen. But it meant that the planet did need to have some sort of defenses. And a population that knew how to fight.

"Today is the first day of training," I told him. "I am supposed to meet the trainees outside the square in the amphitheater. Can you tell me where that is?"

"The amphitheater, yes. It has been a few moons since we held a performance there, but I am glad it is getting use today." The alien's yellow eyes didn't blink as he cut them to the side. "Walk out of the square toward the shallows until you pass through two high pillars. You will see the livestock pens to one side and the stone amphitheater to the other."

I thanked him again, walking where he'd indicated. In the distance, the bright turquoise water of the expansive shallow pools was easy to spot, small boats skimming across the surface. As was indicated by the tea, the planet took much of its bounty from the unusual waters, and most of the food and drink I'd had so far had come from it. As a Vandar who'd been used to plenty of red meat and ale, I had not yet adapted to a diet high in algae and kelp.

"Raas Bron had better hope he does not see me again," I muttered to myself, thinking again about the Vandar life I was missing.

The square was no longer empty as I walked through it, as residents came down from the cave dwellings above and moved around me in a flutter of cloaks. They gave me a wide berth, but I felt their eyes on me, nonetheless.

"Corvak, there you are."

The voice made me stop and turn. I recognized the human male who'd come to my quarters the night I first arrived and the Kimitherian who'd been with him. They were both ministers for the planet and had been the ones to rope me into teaching their males to fight. I didn't know if I was glad to see them, or wished to draw my blade.

"Terel," I greeted the human, turning fully toward them both and squaring my shoulders. Then I nodded to the alien with blue-green scales. "Kerl."

They smiled at me, although the Kimitherian smile looked more strained.

"You are ready to teach our males how to be Vandar warriors?" Terel asked, holding his cloaked hands together so there was no skin showing.

I didn't tell him that it would take more time than I planned to spend on the planet to teach untrained males to fight like Vandar. Since we were trained to wield a blade almost as soon as we could stand and our youth joined raider hordes as apprentices, the Vandar had thousands of hours of battle practice before we ever met an opponent. That would not be the case here. I did not intend to spend the rest of my life on Kimithion III, no matter what the people on the planet thought or Raas Bron had intended.

"I am ready to begin," I said. "Becoming as skilled as a Vandar will take a long time."

"Of course," Kerl said. "We understand."

"But we do have all the time in the world." Terel opened his arms wide. "And the longer you remain on the planet, the longer you will live, as well."

My stomach tightened. The idea of forever on a rudimentary planet away from my fellow Vandar and away from battle made bile rise up in the back of my throat. I swallowed hard, telling myself that this was not permanent. I would find a way back to my people—exile or not.

Kerl cocked his head at me, his yellow eyes unblinking. "He is not used to the idea of so much time."

"I am focused on the task at hand," I said. "And if you truly believe the Zagrath are an imminent danger, we do not have all the time in the world."

Terel and Kerl exchanged a worried look, then the human leader nodded. "You're right, of course. We sometimes forget that the rest of the universe moves faster than we do."

I bit my tongue. I really wanted to ask them how, if they'd lived so long, they hadn't bothered to develop better weaponry or planetary defenses or even better tea, but I reminded myself that I was a guest. Until I got the hell off.

I cleared my throat, aware of many furtive glances darting my way. "I should get to the amphitheater and start my work."

The two males stepped aside and watched me go. I had a feeling most of the aliens in the square were watching me. After all, I did stand a head above the tallest of them.

I hadn't reached the far end of the square when there was a flutter of movement close to me and someone was pressing something warm into my hand. I jumped at the touch, but the person had melted into the crowd by the time I turned around. When I glanced down at the loosely wrapped bundle in my palm and inhaled the scent drifting up from it, I nearly moaned out loud. It was a roll of bread—fresh, yeasty bread—without a trace of green or algae in it.

Without hesitating another second, I jammed the entire thing in my mouth as I scanned the cloaks behind me. I had no idea who had done it, but I wished I could thank them. I hadn't had decent bread since I'd arrived. With the added energy of the roll, I spun around and strode toward the amphitheater.

It was time to teach the males of Kimithion III how to fight like the Vandar. If that was even possible.

CHAPTER TWO

Ch 2

Sienna

I pulled my honey-brown hair up in a bun so tight it tugged at the corners of my eyes. When I flinched from the pain, I released my vise-like grip on my hair.

"Your hair isn't the one you want to hurt," I whispered to my reflection in the warped mirror, meeting my own hazel eyes and glancing quickly away.

No, I wanted to take my anger out on the village delegates who'd decided that only males could learn to fight. Right after I took it out on my father for being so drunk all the time that he didn't care what was happening or pay attention to his two daughters.

Not that my father would have taken my side anyway. When he wasn't drinking the disgusting fermented algae that was the local liquor, he was in lock step agreement with his friends who served as ministers for the planet. He, like them, believed that it was the males who should rule the families and defend the planet, while the females tended the homes and children.

"Yeah, right," I whispered darkly under my breath.

I had no intention of getting married and having a family, especially since I'd seen firsthand how badly that could end up. I opened the top drawer of my dresser, sneaking a peek at the pencil sketch of my mother I hid there. I touched the weathered paper, making sure not to smudge the charcoal lines. Having a family had literally killed my mother, and I had no desire to end up like her—dead and erased.

I slid the drawer shut quietly. My father didn't allow any images of my mother in the house, but I kept this one tucked away so I wouldn't forget what she looked like. The more years that passed from her death, the harder it was to recall her face without the drawing as a reminder. I also hid it so it wouldn't hurt my sister, since my mother had died giving birth to her. No matter how many times I told her that it wasn't her fault, I knew Juliette didn't believe me.

A choked snore from the living room made me stop moving. I held my breath as my father shifted on the couch and then resumed snoring. He'd fallen asleep in the living room after drinking too much—as usual. I honestly didn't know why he even bothered having a bedroom since he never made it to the bed.

Glancing at the sun peeking over the pointy mountain spires and streaming into my window, I groaned. My father would be late for his shift again, not that I was going to dare wake him up.

He didn't like being reminded that he was constantly late for the only job that he could hold on to— cleaning fish down by the shore. It was smelly, disgusting work that few people wanted to do, which meant that they wouldn't fire him when he continued to show upon late or not at all.

I drew in a deep breath. The only advantage to him missing work was that he didn't bring the smell of the shallows back with him. The only scent filling our dwelling now was the aroma of Juliette's bread and baked goods. Although I couldn't hear her in the kitchen, the smell of yeast and sugar told me that she'd been up since before dawn baking. The sunlight also told me that she'd probably already left our dwelling.

My stomach growled, and I hoped she'd saved a roll for me. She usually did, although lately she'd been annoyed with me, and one way she showed her irritation was by not leaving me one of her pastries before taking them down to the village to sell.

Guilt gnawed at me as I turned from the mirror and tugged on my boots. I hated when Juliette was upset with me. Since we were tiny, it had always been the two of us against the world. Or at least against our father. He'd fallen apart after our mother had died and had left us to fend for ourselves most of the time. We'd learned to rely on each other instead of him, and had always been close, despite how different we were.

But lately, she'd been more and more impatient with me. Especially since the Vandar had arrived. My breath caught in my throat when I thought about the huge, muscular alien who'd been exiled to live in our village. Corvak was the name that they whispered in the village square or behind closed doors, and he was so different from anyone I'd ever seen that I couldn't keep my eyes from tracking his every move.

Not that he'd done much moving since he'd arrived. After stalking off the Vandar ship, the bare-chested, tailed alien who wore nothing but a leather skirt and boots, had disappeared into the dwelling he'd been assigned and only emerged once or twice. His rough appearance had caused plenty of whispers, as had the black markings on his chest and the axe he wore on his belt. Neither humans or Kimitherians marked their bodies or carried weapons. We also covered most of our skin, and our males wore their hair short, not long and wild like the Vandar.

Unlike most of the villagers who knew everything about each other, the Vandar had made no effort to socialize. Not that I blamed him. Clearly, he wasn't thrilled to be here, and I heard he'd been reluctant when two of the planet's ministers had asked him to train our males in battle. But he'd finally agreed, and today was the first day of the training.

"And I'm going to be there," I said, pulling a long cloak off a hook near the arched door and throwing it over my shoulders. I didn't care that only the young males of the planet had been invited to train. I was going to show up and hope that the Vandar wasn't as backward as everyone on my planet.

My heart thumped in my chest as I walked from my bedroom to the large room that held the living room, dining area, and kitchen. The ceiling was curved overhead, cut into the gray stone of mountain, with triangular windows looking out toward the path curving down to the square. Sheer curtains flapped in the open windows, keeping out most of the dust but letting in fresh air. Guilt twisted my gut again when I spotted the bunch of thistles in a vase under one of the windows. Juliette tried so hard to make our shabby dwelling look nice while my father did nothing to help, and I used every excuse to stay away as much as I could.

Even though the room didn't smell like fish—courtesy of my father missing work the day before—the scent of the open bottle of fermented algae mingled with the savory smells of baking. I wrinkled my nose as I spotted the lump that was my father flopped across the couch, his bare feet dangling over one end and a scratchy blanket covering the rest of him. Only his unkept, sandy brown hair poked above the covers. My sister had no doubt covered him when she'd gotten up to bake. I could imagine her tiptoeing around the kitchen, trying to mix her batters while not waking him. If he did wake, he wouldn't be grateful that his youngest daughter made enough money with her talent to make up for his lousy and sporadic pay. He would yell at her for being too loud.

I scowled as I thought about his raised voice echoing off the stone of our dwelling, then I spotted the plate of bread on the stone counter, and my anger melted away, replaced by a swell of affection for my little sister. She hadn't forgotten me or decided to punish me.

"Thank you, Juliette," I whispered, snatching one of the golden rolls of bread and taking a greedy bite.

Walking on the toes of my boots, I passed my father without giving him another glance and ducked out the front door. When I was safely outside our dwelling, I polished off the rest of the bread, savoring the pillowy roll as I headed down toward the square. The suns were higher now and mine weren't the only footsteps on the stone path as I rushed around a corner.

"Sienna!"

I grabbed the cloaked figure's arms to keep from knocking her over. Even with the hood shadowing her face, I would know that voice anywhere. "Hey, Juliette."

She threw back her hood and eyed me. "Where are you going?"

I glanced down at her empty basket and tried to change the subject. "You sold out already?"

Even though blonde curls framed her heart-shaped face, she looked anything but angelic at the moment. "Please tell me you're not doing what I think you're doing."

"Okay, I won't tell you." I held her gaze with just as much intensity as she held mine.

Finally, she let out a sigh. "You can't be serious, Sienna."

"Why not?" I crossed my arms over my chest. "Just because I'm a female? It's ridiculous. I'll bet I can fight better than half those boys."

Juliette's blue eyes didn't waver, but she lowered her voice as she glanced around. "Probably, but that doesn't matter. You know what the ministers would say—not to mention our father."

I let out an indignant huff. "He doesn't get a say in what I do. I'll bet the man doesn't even know how old I am."

"He knows you're old enough to get married."

I glared at her. This again? "I've told you. I'm not marrying Donal just because everyone else wants me to."

"But you know what will happen if you reject the son of an important minister." Juliette glanced at the nearest set of windows and pulled me farther away from them.

I did know but I refused to answer her. Instead, I pressed my lips together.

"His family is powerful, Sienna. If you marry Donal, you'd never have to worry about anything for the rest of your life."

Except for Donal touching me, I thought, shivering unconsciously.

"You'd get out of the house," she added.

Juliette knew that was the only thing that could possibly entice me, but still it wasn't enough. "I've told you before. I don't want to marry Donal. I don't love him, and I don't want to be the wife of some minister. If you're so crazy about the idea, why don't you marry him?"

She leaned forward. "He doesn't want me."

"I don't know why not. You're prettier than me, and you can bake." This was true. I had no clue why the arrogant minister's son had set his sights on me, when I had never shown him even a flicker of interest.

Juliette glanced down at herself. "Maybe he doesn't like chubby girls."

"You aren't chubby," I said, an urge to defend my little sister making me almost forget that we were arguing. "Did someone call you that? You've got curves, that's all. I wouldn't mind having some of your curves."

That was also true. While my younger sister was curvy in all the right places—not chubby, thank you very much—I had an athletic build. It was yet another reason I didn't know why Donal had fixated on me. I wasn't particularly girly, and had never bothered trying to be pretty.

Juliette laughed. "Unfortunately, it doesn't work that way. I can't give you some of my curves, and I can't force Donal to like me instead of you."

"Too bad."

My sister's smile faded. "It is. If our family fortunes are dependent on you being a dutiful wife, we're in trouble."

"Our family fortunes are being drunk away every night," I said. "I shouldn't have to sacrifice myself to save the family."

She flinched from my sharp words, and I immediately regretted them, especially since she was the one who did so much to keep us afloat.

"You know I'll do anything for you but *that*," I said.

She nodded. "Who knows? Maybe you'll finally offend Donal enough that he decides he doesn't want you."

"I can't believe I haven't already."

"You're not the only one," Juliette mumbled.

I swatted at her. "Hey!"

Juliette smiled at me, then her expression became serious. "Don't go down there, Sienna. You're only going to be disappointed."

I cut my eyes to the square, which was filling with people. I didn't see the Vandar, but I suspected he was already at the amphitheater. "You don't know that. Corvak might be different. He might not think females are only good for marrying."

Her eyebrow quirked up. "Corvak?"

My cheeks warmed. "I heard some people talking about him. That's his name, isn't it?"

Juliette shrugged but appraised me with narrowed eyes. "I guess. I doubt I'll have much reason to know it. He seems to keep to himself."

"Well, I'll need to know his name. He's going to teach me how to fight like a warrior."

My sister let out another long sigh. "Even if he wanted to, the ministers would never allow it. Females on Kimithion III don't fight."

The reality of her words made my shoulders sag. She was right. Even if the Vandar agreed to it, the ministers never would. And I couldn't even count on my father to take my side. He'd agree with the other males. Then anger flared fresh inside me.

Ever since a small group of human refugees had been allowed to join the native Kimitherians and share the planet, we'd been obliged to follow the established rules and traditions, even though they were stricter than what the original settlers had been used to on Earth. Still, our ancestors had been so grateful to have a planet to share—and one that wasn't overcrowded or stripped of resources like Earth had been—that they agreed to the morality strictures and the male-dominated social structure. It was a trade-off I cursed on a regular basis.

"They'll have to know I'm a female to stop me," I said, flipping my hood up and ducking my head. "This is one time when me not having curves will pay off. No one will know I'm a female in this."

"Sienna—"

I clutched my sister's hands before she could admonish me again. "Please, Juliette. Just don't tell on me. I think this is something I'd do really well. You have your baking, but I don't have anything I'm good at like that. Not yet. I need to know if this is my thing. Please don't tell on me. Cross your heart." I made a criss cross motion over my chest with one finger. "Hope to die."

She shook her head. "You and your vintage Earth sayings." She might not love old Earth slang as much as I did—or feel the need to maintain some sort of connection to our home world—but she still gave me a reluctant smile. "Fine, but only because I won't have to. It's not going to work."

That was good enough for me. "I still have to try." I released her hands and backed away.

"And if father asks where you are?" she called after me.

"You know he won't," I said as I turned, the truth in my words stinging even though it shouldn't have after all this time.

"Sienna," Juliette said, her tone urgent.

I stopped and twisted my head back to meet her gaze. "What?"

She gave me a reluctant grin. "Good luck. If anyone can pull this off, it's you."

I beamed at her, waving as I backed up faster. "Thanks, sis!"

I bustled down the path, bolstered by my sister's encouragement. It wasn't going to be easy. She'd been right about that. Not only did I have to fool the Vandar into thinking I was a male, but I also had to hide my face from all the other fighters.

But I didn't care. My sister believed in me—well, she'd wished me good luck, which was almost the same thing. A laugh of excitement burbled up in my throat, and my heart pounded as I raced down the path getting closer and closer to the village square.

One way or another, I was going to get the Vandar raider to teach me how to fight. And I was going to be the best warrior he'd ever trained. He just didn't know it yet.

CHAPTER THREE

Ch 3

Corvak

I took long steps in front of the males assembled in the dusty amphitheater, my tail swishing behind me. If I hadn't already been regretting my agreement to teach the residents of Kimithion III, I was now. The amphitheater wasn't more than a succession of ringed rows of stone benches surrounding an open area—more of a gladiator ring than anything. But the males assembled in front of me were anything but gladiators.

What did I really expect? They were a nonviolent planet that had no standing army and no defense systems. They'd never been trained to fight or even considered it, despite their long lives.

I squinted into the suns that were above the top of the amphitheater and were now beating down on the cracked ground. I let out a hot breath, inhaling briny air in exchange. It was a hard thing for me to imagine since battle had been my life, but I tried to remind myself that not everyone was Vandar as I appraised the males who'd shown up to be trained.

"Not by a long shot," I whispered, eyeing the shabby and scrawny males lined up in front of me.

There was a mix of humans and Kimitherians, but they all wore cloaks to protect them from the suns, so I only saw glimpses of blue scales or flashes of skin in a variety of shades from beneath drooping hoods. Even with the coverings, it was easy to tell that none of the volunteers were bulky, and I almost instantly gave up on the concept of teaching them to fight with Vandar battle axes. The poor creatures wouldn't be able to lift the heavy iron weapons off the ground.

"Tvek." I cursed under my breath, but noticed a few hoods lifting.

Okay, Corvak, I told myself. *You were battle chief of a Vandar horde. You fought off imperial attacks and coordinated offensive strategies that are still being talked about in hushed tones throughout the galaxy. You can do this.*

"Let's start with a basic assessment," I said, bracing my hands on my hips to face the group. "How many of you have engaged in hand-to-hand combat?"

A few hands went up, but even those seemed unsure. I fought the urge to sigh again. If I was the kind to bet, I would have put money that the combat these males claimed to have seen involved skirmishes with unruly siblings on the living room floor.

"Then we will start at the beginning, so everyone understands the basics of fighting strategy."

"When do we get weapons?" The voice came from the front row, a human male who met my eyes from under his hood. He was one of the taller males, and he appeared to be smirking as he looked at me.

"When you can prove to me you are ready for them," I snapped, glancing away from him.

"What if some of us are ready?"

I swung my gaze back to him. There was always one in every bunch. Too arrogant. Too cocky. When I'd been much younger, that had been me. I thought about my own training as an apprentice on a Vandar horde. The relentless and punishing standards of the Raas and all the raiders had knocked the brazen confidence from me—at least most of it. This human needed to be knocked down a peg or two.

"Why don't you come show me how ready you are?" I beckoned him forward with the flick of my wrist.

Although the human hesitated, he took a few steps forward.

"What is your name, human?" I asked.

He puffed out his chest, what there was to puff out. "Donal."

It was clear this human was somebody on the planet, or thought he was. "Donal." I repeated his name out of respect. "I am Corvak of the Vandar."

"We all know who you are." He flipped his hood back, glancing at the rest if the group and grinning. "You're the exiled Vandar."

A low murmur passed through the group, which I ignored. "That is true, Donal." I stepped closer to him and rested on hand on the hilt of my axe, the feel of the metal familiar and comforting. "Do you know why I was exiled from the Vandar, the most feared and ruthless aliens in the galaxy?"

His smirk had vanished. He shook his head and his brown, wavy hair quivered, even though, to his credit, he remained standing with his shoulders squared.

I grinned widely, leaning closer and dropping my voice. "Excessive use of violence."

He flinched, no doubt wondering how violent you had to be to be considered excessively violent for a Vandar.

I straightened and turned to the group. "But we aren't here to talk about me. You're here to learn how to fight, are you not?"

There was an uneven mumbling of agreement. Nothing like the loud bellowing I would have gotten from my Vandar brothers, but I would take it.

Turning, I unhooked my battle axe from my waist and tossed it at Donal. He grasped the handle, but the weight of it pulled him down to the ground with a loud thud.

I strode over and plucked the weapon off the ground and hoisted him up by the elbow as some of the group stifled laughter. "You should not laugh. I doubt any of you would have done any better." The laughter died instantly. "Weapons are not something to be taken lightly. You will forge your own spears and be trained in them, but only once you've mastered the basics of moving and sparring. Often the difference between life and death is moving swiftly enough to avoid the enemy's weapons. Battle is as much good defense as it is offense."

I waved for Donal to rejoin the group and he walked back, flipping his hood back over his head and covering his flaming cheeks.

"Partner up," I said. "We're going to learn the basics of grappling."

The males shuffled around as they paired off. When there was one straggler left without a partner, I waved him forward to join me at the front.

The flash of blue from under his hood told me he was one of the natives to the planet that looked like bipedal amphibians. The trembling of the cream-colored fabric told me that he was terrified.

"Don't worry," I told him in a low voice. "I have no intention of harming you—or shaming you."

He nodded, but I doubted he believed me. I was speaking the truth though. I'd been shamed enough by my own cruel father to want to shame an innocent like that. Even after so many years, my face heated as I thought of my raider father when he returned from the horde ships with his demands for warrior perfection that had been impossible for a young child to meet. Yet, I had tried valiantly to meet them—only to fail each time.

It had not been a difficult decision to join my uncle's horde, where he was Raas, instead of the one in which my father fought. Yet, it was always my own father, now long dead, whom I seemed to think about when it came time to prove myself. The one Vandar I could never impress was the one I secretly tried to in everything I did. It was why I had always been thirstier for battle and more eager for glory and one of the reasons why exile was so painful.

I pushed thoughts of my father from my mind. It did no good to think about the Vandar now. He had given me nothing but a hunger to prove myself that I could never seem to sate.

"Sir?" The alien's clicking sounds drew my thoughts back to the amphitheater and away from my father. Although the males were standing silently and watching me, they seemed confused by my pause.

I cleared my throat, wishing I'd brought water with me. "Watch me, and follow my motions."

Using the Kimitherian, I demonstrated the basics of deflecting a frontal attack, then a reverse attack without flipping him onto his back. The other pairs started to replicate my moves while I let the Kimitherian practice on me, being careful not to react as I normally would when attacked. After he managed a few attempts that weren't terrible, I thumped him on the back.

"Good work."

His sigh of relief was audible.

As the pairs continued to practice, I walked among them to assess their progress. For the most part, humans had paired with humans and Kimitherians with Kimitherians. Not surprising. Even though the natives to the planet had welcomed the human settlers onto their planet, the species were very different in appearance and temperament. As a Vandar who'd spent his life surrounded by other Vandar, I understood the desire to be with those like yourself, though I couldn't help admiring how well the two peoples coexisted. Of course, the humans were lucky to have found a place after being forced to flee their dying planet—even if Kimithion III was a far cry from what I'd heard about Earth at its peak.

The suns were blazing now, and I understood why the natives were always covered, even though my skin was tough enough to welcome the rays without burning—a carryover from the times when the Vandar roamed the open plains of our home world and lived in the open air.

Despite the heat, the iron hilt of my axe remained cool, and I curled my fingers around it while I paced through the fighters. Although most of their moves were unskilled and lacking in any sort of grace, not all the males were without ability. Donal, who'd had some of the cockiness knocked from him, was one of the stronger males, and he managed to flip his opponent onto the ground.

"Well done," I said, nodding at him as I passed.

He flushed, this time from the compliment, but then my attention was drawn to a pair in the back row, and I moved quickly away to watch them. More specifically, to watch one of them.

The wiry male in a beige cloak moved with impressive speed and flexibility, spinning and parrying away from his opponent before the other male could grab him. Again and again, the one male was thwarted by the other by sheer speed and superior reflexes. Finally, the male who was on the losing end of the grappling session stood and flipped back his hood.

"I give up." He scraped a hand through pale hair. "I can't even catch him."

The opponent stopped moving but didn't remove his cloak, keeping his head lowered.

My pulse quickened at the thought of a worthy opponent, at least when it came to hand-to-hand. "Are you willing to face off against me?"

The cloaked male gave a single nod and lowered himself into a fighting stance. I did the same, sizing up my opponents' size and build. Although the natives were all smaller than me, this man was almost slender, with no bulky muscle stretching the fabric of his cloak.

I lunged, but he spun around the back of me, using my own body to pivot himself away. When I turned and swung my arm wide, he ducked and rolled across the ground, popping up far away from me and resuming his fighting crouch.

"You have an instinctive talent for fighting," I said, moving sideways toward him as he parroted my movement in the opposite direction. He also had a talent for keeping his hood on and lowered just enough so I couldn't see his face, although I'd spotted a flash of skin that was definitely not blue-green scales. "Your moves are mostly defensive though. What happens when you need to strike a blow to your enemy?"

He moved toward me slightly, but it was enough for me to propel myself forward and grasp one of his hands, jerking him off balance and flipping him onto the ground. I pinned his body beneath mine, his face to the dirt and his chest heaving as I lay on him.

"You are an excellent fighter," I said. "For a man. Not yet as compared to a Vandar."

I got off my opponent, pulling him up with me and holding him by his shockingly narrow hips as he regained his balance. I hadn't fought many humans, but this man seemed too lithe. Before he could pull away, I wrapped my tail around his legs to keep him in place and tugged back the hood covering his face.

Correction. *Her* face.

The creature I'd been fighting was a female. Even though her hair was pulled back from her face, her features were decidedly feminine, from her long-lashed, hazel eyes to the curve of her pink lips. I gaped at her without speaking, too shocked that the best fighter in the group was a woman to say anything.

"Thanks for the compliment on my fighting," she said, meeting my gaze with her own defiant one, "but I'm not a man."

CHAPTER FOUR

Ch 4

Sienna

I brushed the dirt off my cloak as the Vandar stared at me. By the time I was done, he was not the only one gaping at me. Most of the other fighters had stopped and gathered around us, apparently just as shocked as Corvak that I was not a male.

"You're a female," Corvak finally managed to say, uncoiling his tail from around my legs. "A human female."

I cocked an eyebrow at him. "Don't let anyone tell you that you're all brawn and no brain."

He frowned at me, clearly not amused. "What are you doing here?"

"Well, I was trying to kick your ass." I shrugged off my cloak, eager to get rid of the extra layer of fabric and to reveal that I was not dressed like a typical female. My dark pants were snug and tapered into my boots, and the pale blue top that extended to my fingertips and up to my throat hugged me like a second skin.

Murmurs rippled through the growing crowd. Most females on the planet wore dresses that covered their ankles, but pants weren't unheard of, although I might have tailored mine a bit tighter than usual. It seemed only fair to ditch my cloak since the Vandar was bare-chested, a fact that was impossible to ignore considering the sweat glistening off his hard muscles and the dark lines swirling across them.

His dark eyebrows lifted. "You wish to train as a warrior?"

Hope blossomed in my chest. Maybe he *was* different. "Don't you think I should? As far as I can see, I'm the best fighter you've got."

His expression was solemn as he studied me then he shook his head. "I agreed to train the males of the planet." His upper lip twitched into a sneer. "Not human females."

Now *that* felt personal. "You have an issue with humans, or females, or is it just the combination that intimidates you, tough guy?"

Before he could respond, the crowd was jostled to the side and Donal appeared.

"Sienna." He took purposeful steps over to me and grabbed my arm. "What are you doing?"

I jerked out of his grasp. "Honestly, I've never had so many people ask me questions that are completely obvious. I'm here to train."

He glanced around him before scowling at me. "This is no place for the woman I plan to marry."

I couldn't help cutting my eyes to the Vandar warrior, who'd crossed his thick arms over his chest and appeared to be watching with some level of amusement. The fact that he was watching all this made my face heat. I turned back to Donal, dropping my voice. "I never agreed to marry you."

He shrugged, as if what I'd said was irrelevant. "You will."

This made the flush of my cheeks become a blaze. "No, I won't. I've told you that I have no desire to be anyone's wife."

Donal spluttered out a laugh. "That's ridiculous, Sienna. What else would you do?"

I hated that there was no good way to answer him. What else would I do if I never married and had a family? I had a very long life to be the village outcast and oddity. I fisted my hands by my sides, aware of all the eyes on me. "I don't know, but I do know that I can't marry you. I don't even know why you'd want to marry me, anyway."

He gave me what I'm sure he thought was a sweet smile, but to me it just looked patronizing and smarmy. "Sienna. You know it's always been you."

I huffed out an exasperated breath. "This isn't the place to discuss this, Donal. We're both here to learn how to fight and defend our planet, and that's what we should do." I pivoted back to Corvak. "Right?"

"The female is correct." The Vandar unfolded his arms and braced them on his hips, making his leather kilt slip down a bit.

My mouth went dry as I noticed the sharp indentation of muscle on both sides of his hips forming a downward-pointing

V. I'd never known males could have muscles like that, and for a moment, I imagined touching the corded ridges of his stomach. Then I tore my gaze away and cleared my throat. "I am?"

He gave a sharp nod. "We've spent too much time watching you two argue. This is a place for training, not personal issues."

"I'm ready to resume training," I said, taking another step away from Donal.

Corvak slid his gaze to me, his long tail twitching. "Not you, female. You need to return to your home."

His words were like a punch to my gut. I stared at him for a moment as they sunk in. "But you said I was excellent fighter."

"That was before I knew you were a female."

I threw my hands up. "Why does that matter? You didn't even know I was a woman until you pulled my hood down. You couldn't tell the difference between me and a man, so why does it matter?"

"I'm sure he could tell the difference," Donal said, giving a conspiratorial look to Corvak. "He was probably just being nice to you, Sienna. Trying not to hurt your feelings."

I didn't deign to look at Donal. He was being such a pathetic suck-up that I wanted to kick him in the teeth. I kept my eyes locked on Corvak.

"No, she is correct," the Vandar warrior said. "I did not know she was a female—until I touched her."

I started at that, watching his cheeks color slightly. My heart was pounding, but instead of it beating from fury, it was something else entirely.

"Oh," Donal stammered, looking back and forth between us. "I didn't know you touched—"

"When I pinned her on the ground," Corvak added quickly. "But that is not the point." His gaze shifted back to mine. "I agreed to teach the males. If females on this planet do not engage in battle, I am not going to be the one to defy that."

"Even if it's a stupid, sexist tradition, and I'm the best fighter you've got?" My fingernails bit into the flesh of my palms as I clenched my hands.

The Vandar crossed his arms again. "Even so."

"I thought the Vandar were the best warriors in the galaxy," I said. "I thought you were the ones who fought against the unjust empire and saved planets that were being oppressed. But you're not even brave enough to stand up to a stupid rule."

A muscle ticked in his jaw as his tail swished rapidly behind him. "It is done." His gaze hardened, all the heat vanishing. "You should go."

Fresh humiliation caused the backs of my eyelids to burn with tears, but I blinked quickly so they wouldn't fall. I wouldn't give the asshole the pleasure of seeing me cry.

I leveled a finger at him. "This *isn't* done."

"Sienna, honey." Donal stepped toward me, his voice dripping with fake concern.

I grabbed his wrist and twisted it hard, bringing him to his knees, then I released him and backed away, shooting a final, scathing glance at the Vandar raider. "Good luck."

I stalked away, pushing through the cloaked males who'd gathered in a tight ring to watch the drama unfold. Even through their hoods, I could feel their disapproving gazes on me, so I threw a few extra elbows to clear the way faster.

Dust caked the toes of my boots once I'd stomped from the amphitheater, but I didn't stop or look up at what I knew were more startled and judgmental faces. I'd left my cloak back in the ring, so I was the only villager not cloaked and hooded as I made my way through the square and up the winding stone path.

I didn't know where I was going, exactly. I didn't care. As long as it was far away from the Vandar raider who'd shown himself to be just as much of a disappointment as every other male in my life. I'd taken the day off work so I could go to the training, not that my boss probably cared. The only reason I'd gotten the job inventorying incoming supplies from off-world transports was because it was mind-numbing work that no one else wanted. It certainly wasn't because I was especially skilled at counting containers. I wasn't great at anything—except fighting.

I'd had to be. I was the only person who could defend my sister against the bullies who seemed to be drawn to her softness, and all the jerks who liked to make comments about our deadbeat dad. I'd learned early on that I was good at fighting. Pretty soon, everyone else had learned it, too. Which was why no one picked on my sister anymore or mentioned our father within earshot of me. Still, as odd as it sounded, fighting was the only thing I'd ever excelled at or took pleasure in doing. When I fought, the world disappeared, and everything seemed to click into place.

"Which was why no Vandar asshole is going to keep me from doing it," I said in what I thought was a whisper, but the wide eyes peering from underneath hoods of passing people told me was not.

When I reached our dwelling, I paused. The last thing I wanted to deal with was my father, although after a stand-off with a real-life, Vandar warrior, I shouldn't be afraid of one drunk.

I walked inside and let out a breath when I saw that the couch was empty and the blanket folded neatly over one arm. There were no sounds except that of my heavy breathing. My father must have stumbled off to work, and my sister was probably visiting a friend a few dwellings away.

My shoulders uncoiled. At least I wouldn't have to explain to Juliette what happened. Having to tell her that I'd been kicked out even though I'd been the best would have been too much. Just thinking about her wide blue eyes filled with sympathy made tears prick my eyelids.

No, I didn't need someone to feel sorry for me. Not now. I hadn't been lying when I'd told Corvak that it wasn't over. I wasn't going to give up so easily. Not when he was the first creature to set foot on the planet who knew anything about warfare or fighting. I finally had a chance to learn how to do something I was good at, and I wasn't going to lose it. I just had to figure out how to convince the Vandar that he was wrong about me.

I let out a slow breath and sank onto the couch, remembering the cold look in his eyes when he'd told me to go. It was going to take something serious to convince him.

An idea teased the corner of my brain, but it made my pulse race just thinking about it. I eyed the half-empty bottle of fermented algae on the coffee table. Lifting it to my lips, I took a reluctant swig, grimacing at the taste but welcoming the burn in my belly.

I was going to need all the liquid courage I could get.

CHAPTER FIVE

Ch 5

Corvak

I watched the female stomp out of the amphitheater with a knot in my belly. *Sienna.* The female who'd fought better than any male in the group, and stood up to me, was called Sienna.

"Return to your sparring," I bellowed, spinning on my heel and the leather of my battle kilt slapping against my thighs. "We are not finished yet."

The pairs resumed grappling, but after seeing Sienna fight, it was almost painful to watch the weak efforts of the others. Even the male who claimed to be engaged to her, Donal, was nowhere near as quick or as graceful.

I thought back to the female's deft moves against me and then to how her body had felt under mine. The instantaneous sense I'd had as soon as I'd pinned her. My tail snapped behind me and my cock twitched, and I clasped my hands in front of myself to keep it from rising. The last thing I needed was to get aroused in an arena filled with human and Kimitherian males.

No, the last thing you need is a complication with a female.

I grunted as I reminded myself why I was exiled to the alien planet in the first place. It had been a human female who had caused all the problems on my horde ship. I'd disdained my fellow Vandar when they'd taken human females to their beds. It had done nothing but weaken them and the horde. So why did I feel drawn to this female?

I strode between the males as they battled with each other, offering corrections and suggestions to improve their stance or their grip. When the group was panting from exertion, their movements sluggish and clumsy, I clapped my hands to get their attention.

"That is all for today. You have progressed well. We will continue tomorrow."

They nodded and muttered thanks as they left the amphitheater, dragging their feet beneath their cloaks. Only Donal remained behind, coming up to me when everyone else had left.

"I'm sorry about that mess with Sienna." He gave me a familiar grin. "You know how it is with women."

"Unless she is a pleasurer, I do not know."

His eyes widened a bit. "A pleasurer? You mean a whore?" He shook his head with vigor. "No, she's definitely not one of those. She won't even give it up to me and, believe me, I've tried."

He gave me another grin, which I didn't return. I did not understand a male who could not convince a female to warm his bed, especially one he intended to be his mate.

"So you've visited a," he hesitated over the word, "pleasurer before?"

"Pleasure planets are common stops for Vandar hordes." I started walking toward the exit, not waiting to see if he followed. "Females are not allowed on our horde ships. Usually."

Donal ran to catch up. "You probably noticed by now that we don't have any pleasurers on Kimithion III. When humans came to the planet as settlers and mixed with the natives, we had to agree to a morality clause. The only relationships between males and females can be through marriage. And our species can't intermarry. It wouldn't work mating-wise, anyway."

I glanced down at him. "Your planet has morality rules that you have tried to defy by bedding the female despite her protests?"

He stammered and coughed, glancing around even though there was no one close enough to hear. "Everyone knows males have needs, right?"

"My needs have never involved an unwilling female."

His face reddened, his eyes hardening for a moment. "She's just playing hard to get. It's a game. She'll accept me. Everyone here marries."

"Everyone on your planet is in mated pairs?" Although Vandar believed in taking mates—and there was one fated mate for each Vandar—we were not restrictive regarding sex. Vandar did not view sex—or enjoying any form of it—as immoral, and it was common to have many partners before finding your one true mate. As a male who'd enjoyed my fair share of exotic alien pleasurers, the idea of the only relationship being marriage seemed choking.

"The ones who've reached maturity. That's why I know Sienna will come around eventually." He swiped a hand across his sweaty forehead. "What other option does she have? Stay unmarried and unmated for her entire life?"

Considering how long the residents of the planet lived, that did seem like a grim fate.

"There must be more eager females," I said to him, as we passed through the arched entrance to the amphitheater and headed toward the village square. The scent of saltwater and fish wafted up from the shores of the shallows, making my nose twitch.

Donal waved a hand. "She's just playing hard to get. It's part of our dance."

I looked at him askance. "If you say so."

"Besides," Donal dropped his voice as we approached a group of people walking toward us. "Sienna would be a fool to reject a match with me, especially considering her family and her lousy job. She should be grateful I would consider marrying a female who is content doing inventory for the supply chief."

I slowed my pace as I mentally noted that Sienna worked with the department that handled incoming off-world supplies. "What is wrong with her family?"

He twitched one shoulder. "Her mother died when her younger sister was born, and her father never got over it. He spends most of his time drinking their money away. Sienna got to be so scrappy because she fights anyone who says anything bad about her father or sister." He chuckled. "She even punched me in the nose once for saying her sister was as doughy as her yeast rolls."

I was liking this human less and less. "Maybe that is why she doesn't wish to marry you."

"That was forever ago. Besides, if she rejected everyone who ever said something about her family, there would be no one left on the planet."

We reached the obelisk in the center of the village, and I stopped. "Why are you telling me this?"

"Just so you don't feel bad about kicking her from your training. She should know better than to do the things she does, but she does them anyway." He shook his head as if he was talking about a naughty child. "Her temper is something I'll teach her to control once we're married."

Good luck with that, I thought. I would have bet good money that Sienna would never tame her temper or marry this weak man.

I flicked my gaze over him. "Let's hope the rest of the males in the training improve quickly, or your planet is in real trouble. She remains the best fighter I saw today."

With that, I turned and strode through the square and started up the winding stone path cut into the mountain. For some reason, the man's words about Sienna had gotten under my skin. I might have just met the woman, but I didn't like how Donal talked about her, or how he'd attempted to claim her as his, despite her obvious distaste for him. It flared a possessive streak in me that made no sense.

I stomped my boots as I walked, my head down, even though the sun was also lower and no longer glinting in my eyes. Why did I care if Donal wanted to lay claim to Sienna? I was a newcomer on the planet and didn't understand their ways. Maybe he was right, and she would be foolish to reject him.

But maybe she doesn't care, I thought. The woman who'd been brave enough to pretend to be a male so she could learn to fight would not bow to rigid customs. It was clear she was a rebel, and as a member of a species who'd spent millennia rebeling against the rule of the empire, I admired her spirit. My heart beat faster as I remembered the feel of her hips as I held her. It had been the curve of her flesh that was softer than any man's hip that had tipped me off that she was no male.

I ignored the flush of pleasure the memory provoked. It didn't matter that she had a spirit I admired, or that she was the best fighter I'd seen. I couldn't go against the planet's traditions if I was to live among its community—which meant I couldn't let Sienna in the training, and I definitely couldn't wonder what her hair would look like when it wasn't pulled up high, or what it would be like to peel her snug-fitting clothes off her body.

I growled low and sidestepped to avoid running over a pair of native Kimitherians walking toward me as they chattered in their native tongue. "Sorry."

My gruff apology sent them scurrying away even faster. Great. The villagers were clearly scared of me, and the intense training session I'd subjected the males to wouldn't do much to improve my reputation. I pushed open the door to my dwelling and stormed inside. I tugged off my boots, took off my wide belt, and propped my battle axe by the door before collapsing onto the stiff couch and huffing out a breath.

At least I was finally alone. All I wanted to do was have something to eat and collapse into bed. "And if I'm lucky, I'll wake up and discover this has all been a horrible nightmare."

I closed my eyes and leaned my head back. That was when I heard it.

My eyes flew open. I was *not* alone.

CHAPTER SIX

Ch 6

Sienna

As soon as he barreled into his dwelling and started to undress, I knew I'd made a huge mistake. The fermented algae drink that I'd gulped down at home was starting to wear off, and the liquid courage that had convinced me to sneak into his dwelling was now morphing into full-fledged panic.

I rubbed my head and attempted to quiet my breath. What had I been thinking? How could I have possibly thought that crawling through Corvak's window and lying in wait for him to return was a good idea?

When he unhooked his wide belt and let it fall to the floor, I squeezed my eyes shut. If he dropped his kilt, he'd be naked, and then I might legitimately pass out—and not only because I'd drunk way too much.

It had all made sense when I'd been at home swigging down the bitter dregs of the liquor my father had left behind. As the warmth had spread through my body, sending tingles down my arms and making my lips go numb, the plan had seemed foolproof. All I needed to do was get some one-on-one time with the Vandar. That way I could convince him to teach me without Donal interrupting and making me look bad. I could also explain about Donal and how delusional he was. For some reason, I hated the idea of the Vandar thinking I was promised to the man.

All I needed to do was sneak into Corvak's dwelling and wait for him to get home. Then I could have a rational conversation with him and fully explain why I should learn to fight and why he should be the one to teach me. Once he'd heard my arguments, he'd be sure to agree with me. At least that had been what my booze-addled brain had thought before I'd been standing flattened to the wall of his short hallway and wishing I was anywhere else.

When Corvak flopped down on the couch, I opened one eye. He was facing away from me, and I could see his thick thighs bulging out between the leather strips of his skirt as he stretched his long legs out in front of him. At least he was still wearing something. He tipped his own head back and closed his eyes.

This was it. My chance to escape without being seen. I cut my eyes to the window I'd entered from. All he'd have to do would be glance to the side to spot me, but maybe if I was extremely stealthy, I could crawl out without him waking.

I let out a small sigh, which I immediately regretted.

The Vandar raider's eyes popped open, and his entire body tensed.

No no no no no no no. I held my breath and pressed my body even harder into the wall and the shadows of the hallway. Fear had sharpened my mind and banished any remnants of my buzz, my heart hammering so loudly in my chest I was sure he could hear it from where he sat.

Before I could risk taking a breath, Corvak leapt to his feet, moving with the grace and speed of a predator and vaulting over the back of the couch in a single, smooth movement. Within moments, he'd reached me and flipped me around so that my face was pressed into the wall and my arms were pinned over my head. His huge body held mine in place, his mouth to my ear.

"Who are you?" He bit out the words. "What are you doing here?"

I'd had the wind knocked from me when he'd slammed himself against may body, so I sucked in a shaky breath. "It's me. Sienna. From the training."

The pressure on my hands relaxed as he stepped back and spun me around to face him. He kept my hands over my head and his arms braced over me holding them. His dark eyes were wild, and he looked every bit the terrifying raider he was supposed to be.

"What are you doing in my quarters?"

I strained against his grip, but he was too strong. "If you let me go, it might be easier to have a conversation."

He didn't make a move to release me. "If you truly wanted a conversation, why were you waiting for me like a thief?"

I jerked in his grasp, thrashing where I stood. "I'm not a thief!"

"An assassin then?" He eyed me warily. "Maybe you came to punish me for not allowing you to train with the group?"

I stopped my fruitless struggling and tilted my head at him. "Why would I kill the one person who can teach me to fight?"

He didn't look convinced by my words, his full lips pressed together, and his brow furrowed. Even though his face looked even more menacing in the shadows of the hallway, I had an urge to touch him and run my finger down the scar slashing his cheek. But I had a stronger urge to punch him in the gut.

I jerked my gaze back to his. "If I came here to kill you, where is my weapon?" I pinned him with a sharp look. "Even I'm not cocky enough to think I could kill a Vandar with my bare hands."

He shifted his hold on my wrists to one of his large hands, using the other to move deftly down my body. His fingers skimmed down each arm and then across my breasts and stomach.

I bucked against him. "What the hell do you think you're doing?"

"Searching you for weapons." His voice was a dark purr, as his hand slid around my back and down the curve of my ass. "Spread your legs."

My breath caught in my throat. "What? No." I glanced down. "Even your arm isn't *that* long. Trust me. I don't have any weapons strapped to my legs."

"I don't plan to use my arm, and I do *not* trust you."

When I felt something move up the outside of my calf, unwanted shivers of pleasure made me twitch. He was feeling me up with the tip of his tail. I bit my bottom lip to keep from moaning as his tail slipped between my legs and moved higher. His eyes were pools of darkness, his gaze never leaving mine as his tail slid over my body and finally coiled around my waist.

I released the breath I'd been holding. "I told you I wasn't armed. I didn't come to kill you. I came to talk to you."

His eyes held me for a moment longer before he dropped my wrists and stepped back, although his tail remained around my waist, keeping me from moving away from the wall. "I wasn't aware we had anything more to discuss."

Now that he wasn't on top of me, it was easier to breathe, and my heart wasn't beating like a tripwire. It would be a lie to say that my pulse had stopped fluttering at the sight of the massive Vandar looming over me, black marks etched across the hard swell of his chest muscles. But then the indignation I'd felt after he'd kicked me from the training flashed fresh in my mind. "You know I was the best fighter out there today."

"I never said you weren't."

I rubbed at my wrists, the skin still buzzing from the heat of his flesh against mine. "Then why won't you train me? I thought the Vandar were all about being the best warriors in the galaxy. Well, I'm the best. At least, on Kimithion III."

"But your planet doesn't allow females to fight. I would be going against the code if I allowed you in the training." He scraped a hand through his long hair. "I don't know if you've noticed or not, but I'm a guest on your planet. And not a very welcome one."

For the first time I thought about what it must be like for him when all the villagers stared at him or moved away when he approached. I knew what it was like to feel like you didn't belong. "*I'm* glad you're here. You're the most exciting thing that's ever happened to our planet."

He choked back a rough laugh. "Then I feel sorry for your planet."

"You should. Nothing ever changes here. We might live forever, but we're stuck in a backwards existence where everyone has certain roles and no one can ever do anything different or be anything that's unexpected, and we can never leave."

Something flickered behind his eyes. "I'm not sure what you think I can do about that."

My shoulders slumped. "Nothing. I don't expect you to do anything about it. I know you can't. You may be a badass Vandar warrior, but you're not magic."

The corners of his mouth quirked up. "Thank you, I think."

"All I'm asking is that you teach me to fight. I know I'm good at it. It's the only thing I've ever been truly good at. It's the only thing I've ever loved doing."

He angled his head at me. "You love fighting?"

I nodded. "When I'm fighting it feels like the world slows down, and it's just the beating of my heart and the movements of my body. It's like some kind of outside force takes over, and I instinctively know what to do."

He grunted and his tail tightened around my waist. "You sound like a Vandar."

"Thanks. That's the nicest thing anyone's ever said to me. Usually people here think I use too many old Earth phrases."

One of his dark eyebrows lifted. "Donal doesn't say sweet things to you?"

My face warmed, but it was anger that flushed my cheeks, not arousal. "I will never marry Donal, no matter what he says." I spit out each word.

"I believe you." Corvak uncoiled his tail from my waist and turned from me. "Unfortunately, he doesn't believe that."

I put my fingers to my waist, already missing the warmth of his tail. "It doesn't matter what he thinks. No matter how important his father is, he can't force me to marry him. I'd rather die."

Corvak walked a few steps and spun around to face me. "It's shocking you aren't Vandar. Still, I didn't come here to get embroiled in domestic disputes or cause a scandal by teaching a female to be a warrior." He held up a hand. "No matter how good she is. Even your presence would cause a disturbance, like it did today. That will not make it easier for me to prepare your people to defend themselves against the empire. And that is my priority."

I opened my mouth to argue with him, then I stopped. He was right. The community would never allow me to train with the males. I'd been a fool to think they would and a stubborn idiot to try.

"Okay, Vandar," I said, walking over to stand in front of him and crossing my arms over my chest, fighting to keep my gaze from drifting to the dark lines curling across his bare chest. "Then I have a proposal for you."

CHAPTER SEVEN

Ch 7

Corvak

I peered down at the female standing in front of me with her arms folded over her chest and her eyes flashing. It took all my restraint not to curl my tail around her again and feel the warmth of her body. "What kind of proposal? I have no intention of taking you as a mate so you can escape Donal."

She scowled at me. "Don't flatter yourself, tough guy."

I almost laughed. I was used to people cowering from me, but this female did not seem scared of me at all. Was I losing my touch? I growled, curling my lip in an attempt to intimidate her. "Do I need to remind you that you have no leverage with me, female?"

She lifted her chin. "Sure I do, you just don't know it yet."

I raked a hand through my hair. This female was nothing but an irritation I didn't need and a distraction I could not afford. Although I now understood the attraction one could feel towards human females, they were still nothing but trouble for a Vandar. "What is your proposal? Tell me, before I grow weary and throw you out the door."

Her gaze flickered to the arched door then back to me. "Fine. My proposal is that you teach me how to fight." She held up a hand before I could interrupt. "Privately."

I stared at her. "You mean secretly."

"Well, yeah. Obviously, no one could know."

Now that we were no longer in the dim hallway and stood in my small living area, my gaze was drawn to her hair. It was still pulled up into a tight knot on her head, but it was the most fascinating shade of golden brown, with strands of red and gold glinting in the flickering light.

"Well?" Her sharp question made me pull my gaze away from her hair and my urge to unknot it and watch it fall loose.

I mimicked her crossed arms with my own. I had no intention of granting her proposal, but I was curious to hear her reasoning. "How exactly do you envision I could train you secretly? My quarters aren't large enough, and I doubt yours are either."

She shook her head. "We'd have to do it outside the village and at night."

"At night?" Now I was intrigued. "You wish us to sneak away from the village at night? Don't you think someone will notice us creeping around?"

She gave me a pointed look. "We wouldn't leave the village together obviously. We'd have to time it right, but most villagers are in their dwellings after the evening meal. I don't know if you've noticed or not, but this planet is pretty dull, especially after the suns go down. Most families play games in their dwellings and occasionally there's a performance in the amphitheater, but people aren't usually out after dark."

I returned her look. "And your sister and father? Won't they notice you missing at night? You don't play games?"

Her expression darkened. "We aren't one of those types of families. My father won't notice, and my sister will cover for me."

"You've thought this through." I leaned forward so that she had to tip her head back to continue to meet my gaze. "But you haven't told me yet what's in it for me."

She opened and closed her mouth. "What do you mean?"

"You've told me why this is important for you and how you think the logistics can work, even though I'm not sure if you've thought through every contingency, but you've yet to explain why I'd give up my evenings and risk my good standing in the community to sneak around with you."

Color suffused her cheeks. "You wouldn't be sneaking around with me. You'd be teaching me and helping the planet defend itself."

I shrugged one shoulder, enjoying watching her outrage grow. "I'm already doing that during my training during the day. It's a pretty big ask to want me to conduct another entire training session for one person."

Her hazel eyes narrowed. "I didn't know it would be too taxing for a big, tough Vandar like you but if you don't have the stamina…"

I huffed out a laugh, and let my gaze drift down her body. "You are worried about my stamina, female?"

She swallowed and the pink in her cheeks became blotchy patches of red. "No. I don't care anything about your stamina. I thought you might want to teach me out of the goodness of your heart."

"I'm an exiled Vandar battle chief," I growled. "There is no goodness in my heart."

"I don't believe that." Her voice trembled as she spoke.

"Believe what you wish, female." I wrapped my tail around the back of her legs. "But do so at your own risk."

She blinked rapidly as she looked up at me. "Fine. If you won't teach me out of the goodness of your heart or because you want to ensure that my planet is as prepared as possible to fight off the empire, then you should do because you don't want me showing up in your dwelling every night for the rest of your exile on this planet."

"What?"

She grinned, her voice stronger. "You heard me, tough guy. If you refuse to teach me, I'm going to keep after you until you wished you just agreed to it in the first place." She held up one hand and started counting off her fingers. "I'm going to dog your steps. You won't be able to go anywhere without me following you. And you'll never know when I'll be waiting for you in your dwelling, or maybe I'll sneak in and wake you up every morning. You do like to wake to loud singing, don't you? Or maybe you'd rather fall asleep to singing. I can always yodel you to sleep."

As I studied the female's face, I knew she was serious. And although I didn't know what "yodeling" was, I did not want to find out. Part of me wanted to string her up by her ankles and another part of me admired her tenacity.

"I would give my kingdom for an *oblek* right now," I said through gritted teeth while she smiled up at me. "You are truly a malevolent creature, do you know that?"

"I told you I had leverage."

I grunted. "I will admit that you have the cunning of a Vandar, and the heart of a warrior. I will agree to your proposal if only to keep you from harassing me."

She jumped up and threw her arms around my neck. "Thank you!"

I stiffened at her embrace. I was not used to females embracing me unless they were well-paid, and then their embraces were more practiced and less exuberant. Heat coiled in my core as her body pressed against me, and my tail instinctively slid up the back of her leg.

Then she dropped her arms and backed away, her eyes wide. "Sorry. I was excited and got carried away."

My tail released her and then twitched in frustration, mirroring my internal turmoil.

Sienna continued backing up until she'd reached the door, but before she opened it, I advanced on her, leaning one hand against the door so she couldn't open it. I towered over her, my chest heaving.

"You have given me your proposal. Now hear my terms."

She bit her plump bottom lip, all traces of excitement gone as she nodded mutely.

"This will be our secret," I continued, my voice a deadly rumble. "Tell no one. I will give you no special treatment because you are a female. I will train you just as hard and ruthlessly as I do the males. Maybe even more so because you want this so badly. And when your body aches and you want to beg me for mercy, don't. I won't suffer your complaints. You wish to be trained like a Vandar raider? This is what you should expect."

The hazel of her eyes had been almost entirely swallowed up by the black pupils as she stared at me without blinking or looking down. "I agree to your terms, Vandar."

"Good." I shifted my hand on the door down so that it was just above her shoulder and I leaned in so that my lips brushed her ear. "There is one more matter to settle."

"Okay," she whispered, shivering from my touch. "What is it?"

I inhaled the scent of her skin as I curled my tail around her ankle, letting my eyes close as I fought every primal urge roaring through my body. "The matter of payment."

CHAPTER EIGHT

Ch 8

Sienna

My knees almost buckled. "Payment?"

His whispered words skated down my spine and sent frissons of desire arrowing through me as the furry tip of his tail circled my ankle.

"This should be a fair exchange, don't you think? And you agreeing *not* to torment me isn't a fair payment, although it is appreciated."

I drew in a sharp breath, wishing I wasn't pinned against the door. "I don't have anything to give you. My family has no money, unless you wish to be paid in my sister's pastries."

He hummed, shaking his head slightly. "I was not thinking of pastries, although I suspect I now know who to thank for the warm roll this morning. But you have something I *do* want."

I held my breath, steeling myself for what was coming. I'd had Donal's eyes on me enough to know what male desire felt like, although being close to Corvak was an entirely different proposition than being close to Donal. The Vandar's closeness made it hard for me to breathe, and every place he touched on my skin felt scorched. Donal only made me cringe.

Despite Donal's persistence, I'd never been alone with him—or with any male. Our society didn't allow for males and females to be alone if they weren't married, at least not in any interesting way. So, like every female on my planet who was unwed, I was also untouched.

But, like all the other rules imposed on me, I didn't care about breaking it.

"Now?" I asked, my heart racing.

He leaned back and met my gaze. "Now what?"

I attempted to keep my voice from quivering. "Do you want to do it now, or after we've started the training?"

He studied me for a moment, cocking his head and then taking a big step back. "I think you misunderstand me, Sienna. I don't want from you what you think I do."

I locked my knees to keep from sliding down the door and onto the floor. "What?"

His gaze raked me up and down. "As appealing as you are, I have no intention of claiming your body as payment."

Relief flooded me, then a twinge of regret. "Oh." I steadied my breath and put my hands on my hips, a little irritated that he'd made me think he was about to fuck me up against the door. "Then what do you want?"

"I want you to help me get off this planet."

It took a moment for the words to sink in, then I shook my head as if to dislodge them. "But you just got here." I leveled my gaze at him. "And you just agreed to my deal, which was to teach me how to fight. How are you supposed to do that if you aren't on the planet?"

He turned, crossed the living area, and entered the galley kitchen. "Don't worry, female. I have no intention of leaving right away. I will fulfill my promise to your leaders and to you. I will teach you all to fight and defend yourselves against the empire. But then I must go." He opened a cabinet and pulled down a wrapped bundle. "I can't spend the rest of my life here, even if I was exiled."

I couldn't exactly fault him, since I'd just railed against my planet. Kimithion III was no place for a Vandar warrior, or anyone who bristled against rules.

I walked over and stood on the other side of the beige-stone counter as he fumbled with the wrapped food. "Where will you go, if you're exiled from the Vandar?"

Corvak pulled a flattened strip of seaweed from the bundle and offered it to me first. I waved it off then he took a bite. "I was only exiled from one horde, not the entire species. If I cannot join another horde, I will join the Valox resistance. If that fails, I'll become a solo guerrilla fighter. Anything to keep battling the empire."

I admired his intensity and his devotion to the Vandar cause of destroying the empire. "Okay, so how do I come into it? I don't know anything about any of the things you just mentioned."

He chewed the crunchy seaweed, grimacing as he swallowed. "Maybe not, but you do inventory the arriving supplies from off-world, don't you?"

"Yes," I answered hesitantly. How did he know that? Had he been asking around about me?

"Then you're just the person who can help me stow onto a supply transport ship when it's time for me to go."

As much as I dreamed about leaving Kimithion III, I'd never thought of stowing away on a supply ship. Mostly because I'd never leave my sister behind, but also because I'd never set foot off my planet. As much as I liked using old Earth slang, I couldn't even imagine what it was like somewhere other than Kimithion III.

"So? Do we have a deal? You will help me leave when it is time, and I will teach you to fight like a Vandar?"

I nodded. For some reason, though, the thought that he was already plotting his escape from the planet stole some of the satisfaction from my victory. "We have a deal."

It was better this way, I reminded myself. The Vandar didn't fit in here, and he never would. He'd be just as miserable as I was if he had to stay, and I wouldn't wish an eternity of drudgery and boredom on anyone. Corvak was never meant to stay forever, so it was good that I got used to the idea of him leaving now. Even if he was the most interesting thing that had ever happened to the planet or ever would happen.

"So," I said, coming around the counter. "Who told you about my glamorous job?"

"Your future mate was more than eager to tell me about it."

I shot him a deadly look. "I told you, I'm never going to marry him."

The Vandar's lips twitched. "I'm glad to hear it. I do not like him very much."

"You and me both," I mumbled, as I joined him in his kitchen. "Don't you have anything to eat aside from dried seaweed?"

He glanced at the food packet then at me. "Is there anything to eat here *but* dried seaweed or algae or fish?"

I rolled my eyes. "You're eating Kimitherian food. You should be eating human food. I can't believe no one explained this to you." I took the seaweed from him. "The species native to this planet evolved from amphibians, so they love anything that comes from the water. To be honest, the shallows provide us with a lot of protein between the fish, algae and kelp. It's not bad for you, it's just not the tastiest thing in the world—unless you're Kimitherian. When humans came, we planted crops and berries and brought some small livestock. We also get supplies like grain from off-world trading. There are a couple of shops in the village that deal in food you'll prefer."

"This place is very different from a Vandar warbird." He let out a sigh that was sadder than anything.

"I'll bet." I put my hand into my pocket and pulled out a slightly flattened roll. "Eat this. My sister is the best baker in the village. I'll make sure she keeps you stocked up with the good stuff."

His eyes widened and a smile teased the corner of his mouth. "You always keep bread in your pockets?"

"Do you want it or not?"

He looked down at the seaweed then snatched the bread from me. "Oh, I want it."

I watched him take ravenous bites and then turned and headed for the window. "We should start tomorrow night. I'll send you a time and place with tomorrow's bread delivery." I swung a leg through one of his windows. "Catch you later."

"What are you doing?"

"Going out the same way I came in." I winked at him. "I don't think either of us wants me being seen walking from your dwelling after dark. Around here, no one would ever believe that a male like you would be able to control himself around a helpless female. No offense, but they think you're a bit of a brute. Not that I believe that."

He eyed me as I swung my other leg up. "You should be careful, female. They might be more right about me than you are."

CHAPTER NINE

Ch 9

Corvak

I watched her disappear from the windowsill, her head ducking through the triangular hole in the stone, followed by her leg. The thin curtain flapped back in place and the room was silent, leaving no trace that the female had been in my quarters.

Good, I thought, turning on my heel and striding toward the small bathing chamber in the back. If I could, I'd forget she'd ever been there as well.

Lowering my head to pass under the top of the arched doorframe, I unhooked my battle kilt and let the heavy leather fall to the floor, slapping the stone sharply. Light from the moons shone into the small room from an open skylight, giving enough of a glow that I could see to flick on the water for the shower. I didn't wait for the water to heat, instead plunging myself under the cool cascade and sucking in a breath.

I flattened both palms against the stone wall and let the water flow across my back. Even the slightly salty scent of the water didn't bother me. At least the village had freely running water in all the homes as well as lights and power. Not completely primitive after all. But not a place I wished to live out the rest of my days.

I closed my eyes, forcing myself not to think about my exile and how long I would be stuck on Kimithion III. The last thing I needed was to rehash the impulsive actions that had landed me on the planet. No, that was wrong. The absolute last thing I needed was a secret pact to teach one of the females to fight.

I growled and tipped my head up so the water—now tepid—could beat on my face. What had I gotten myself into?

Thoughts of the human female made me growl again and my cock swell. I turned away from the water and dragged both hands through my wet hair. I had no interest in a female, especially not a human one who used strange phrases and climbed through windows.

My lip curled at the thought of my fellow Vandar warriors and the human women they'd claimed. Females made you weak and distracted you from what was important—battle. It was why none were allowed on a Vandar horde. That is, until Raas Kratos had taken one as a spoil of war. I'd been against it when he'd taken his future mate, and I'd been against it when Raas Bron had taken a female onboard. The female he'd taken was why I was exiled.

"And why I have no desire for a human," I said, my words echoing in the circular stone shower.

Then why did Sienna's image keep popping into my brain? Why was my cock aching as I remembered the feel of her body pressed against mine, her eyes wide as she looked up at me? When she'd thought that my price for teaching her was fucking, those hazel eyes had grown dark. But it hadn't been fear I'd seen. Not entirely. There had also been heat there—and desire. She would have paid that price.

I shook my head and droplets of water scattered across the walls. Not that I would ever force a female. The thought was repellent. I was a Vandar. We did not force females. We did not have to. If we needed release, we paid handsomely for the services of pleasurers, and I did not know of a single raider who didn't ensure that the females had as good a time as they did. Just like there was no such thing as a solo victory, there was no true pleasure if it was not shared.

Well, almost none. I let my gaze fall to my cock jutting out from my body, the dark lines that matched the ones on my chest swirling boldly down the shaft. Fisting the base, I closed my eyes again. I wanted to think about the winged Haralli pleasurers or the Felaris twins who worked in tandem, but as much as I tried to recall four hands eagerly moving across my bare flesh, it was Sienna's face that filled my mind.

Tvek. What was it about the female that drew me in like a *carvoth* to a flame? She certainly wasn't practiced at the art of seduction. Actually, she didn't make any attempts to be feminine or alluring at all. Yet she was beautiful without trying, and she had a spirit and love for battle that I shared.

I stroked my hand up and down as I remembered the way she'd moved in the amphitheater, graceful and swift. Then I remembered the curve of her hips when I'd held her, and the jolt of awareness that she was not male. I almost laughed. No, Sienna was definitely not a male. I'd felt that when I braced my body against hers, the swell of her high breasts heaving as she'd breathed. And her scent.

My body shuddered as I recalled the warmth of her skin as I'd inhaled the smell of her neck. Even though she'd been battling under the suns, her skin had held the faint aroma of sugar, making it almost impossible not to want to lick her.

Stroking my hand faster up and down my rigid length, I imagined tasting her, running my tongue across her soft skin and hearing her moan in response. Sienna would not be a shy girl afraid to make a sound. She was bold and fearless in life, and she would be the same way in bed. Thinking of Sienna in my bed, her arms and legs wrapped around me, and my hands fisted in her honeyed hair while she moaned and writhed was too much. Then I imagined pleasuring her with my tail. My cock jerked as my entire body convulsed from the sudden rush of release. Black spots danced in front of my eyes from the onslaught of pleasure, wave after wave hitting me. I threw back my head and roared, the stone reverberating as my cock pulsed hot onto the floor of the shower.

When I was spent, I stood shaking under the warm water, cursing my weakness. I could not afford to think of the human female that way. Not if I wanted to get off the planet and back to raiding. Sienna might stir my desire, but she was nothing but a dangerous distraction, as were all females—especially human ones.

As the buzz from my release faded, I flipped off the water and snatched a towel off a nearby hook. I could not afford to fall into the trap my Vandar brethren had. Obsessing over a female could lead to nothing but more pain for me; and being stuck on Kimithion III for even longer than I needed to be, that was unacceptable.

I toweled myself roughly, gritting my teeth. I couldn't go back on my deal. I'd agreed to it, and Vandar did not go back on their word. Besides, I needed her help to escape. But I could not allow myself any more weakness. Not when it came to Sienna. Not only would it be bad for me, but any contact between us was also strictly forbidden by her planetary customs. As backward as they were, I did not want to buck them when I was living as a guest in their community. Being exiled twice was not appealing.

I glanced back at the stone shower. My fantasies about the human would have to remain just that. Nothing could ever happen between me and the female.

I stomped off to bed, praying to the gods of old that Sienna did not haunt my dreams.

CHAPTER TEN

Ch 10

Sienna

As soon as I stepped inside our dwelling, I knew. My insides turned the consistency of jellied algae when I heard his voice.

"Where have you been?"

I pulled the door closed behind me and squared my shoulders as I turned. Just my luck that my father would be home when I returned. I could usually count on him staggering in long after I'd gone to sleep, but today I wasn't so fortunate.

"Out," I said, knowing that my reply would only stoke his anger, but not caring.

My father sat on the couch, his elbows on his knees and his hands clasped in front of him. His sandy brown hair was still unkempt, and the pervading scent of fish told me he'd been to work. Although his eyes were bloodshot, he looked more sober than usual. More bad luck for me.

"I heard what you did." Even though his voice was quiet, it trembled with anger.

I bit back a smart-ass response about me being shocked he knew anything about me. It wouldn't do me any good to enrage him more. Instead, I met his gaze and remained silent.

He held my eyes for a few moments, then looked away. "Did you really think you'd get away with it? Trying to be like one of the males?"

"I wasn't trying to be like a male. I just wanted to learn to fight."

"Like a male," my father said. "You know females on Kimithion III don't do such things. It's never been done."

"Which is a stupid reason. I was the best fighter out there, male or female."

Now my father stood. "I also heard that Donal had to step in."

My face heated as I thought about Donal and how he'd treated me like I was his property. "He didn't *have* to do anything. I was handling myself just fine."

My father rubbed a hand over his face. "Your actions shame him, Sienna. Don't you see that? No husband wants his wife running around acting like a man."

"I'm not his wife."

He threw his arms open wide. "You will be. Unless you ruin everything."

"I've told you before, but maybe you were too hungover to remember." I folded my arms tightly in front of me. "I'm not marrying Donal."

His face reddened and he advanced on me. "You *will* marry Donal."

When I was younger, I would have shrunk from him barreling toward me. But now, I was just as tall as him. Now, I could take him in a fight. I drew myself up to my full height and dropped my arms to my sides, balling them into fists.

Out of the corner of my eye, I saw Juliette enter the living area from the hallway, her face pinched as she wrung her hands. She hated when we argued, which was why I usually went to great lengths to avoid him.

He stopped, glancing at Juliette then back at me and taking in my stance. "You would hit your own father?"

I clenched my fists tighter. "You would force your daughter to marry someone she hates?"

He hesitated for a moment, clearly sizing me up, then he turned and waved a hand dismissively at me. "You don't know what you want. You're still a child."

"I'm past the age of maturity, and I know that I will never marry Donal. I don't care what you do to me. I won't spend hundreds of years with that man."

My father turned back to me, his face twisted. "You'd rather spend hundreds of years alone? Like me?"

I knew he meant that he would spend the rest of his life without my mother. Juliette choked back a sob, and I glared at him. "At least you picked each other."

He sank back down on the couch, putting his head in his hands. "And I still lost her. Making a choice doesn't mean anything. It's all a game of chance." He peered up at me through bleary eyes. "You have just as much of a chance of being happy with Donal as you do with anyone. And this way you'll be secure and taken care of. You'll never have to worry about anything being married to a minister's son. None of us will."

And there it was. For the briefest moment, I'd thought he might actually be thinking about my future, but it all came down to him. If I married Donal, he'd be better off. The father-in-law of a minister's son would never be allowed to work at the shore. He'd probably be given a cushy job he wouldn't even have to do. Or maybe Donal would support him entirely. Bile rose in the back of my throat.

"Sorry I'm ruining all your grand plans," I spat.

His eyes narrowed. "Your mother would be ashamed of you."

Juliette sucked in a breath and then held it as no one spoke. We never mentioned my mother—he didn't allow it—so the shock left us all speechless. When I allowed myself to breathe again, my chest ached, the physical pain almost making me double over.

I thought of the picture of my mother tucked away in my drawer, her eyes kind and her smile bright. I didn't remember much about her, but I did know that she'd loved me. Snatches of memories floated through my mind of her singing to me and kissing my stomach as I giggled. I would not let him stain what memories I had left.

"You think she would be ashamed of *me*?" I asked, my words cold and cutting as I leveled a hard, unforgiving gaze at him.

The fury on his face morphed into shock and then fear, as if he was seeing me for the first time and realizing that I wasn't afraid of *him*. Standing quickly, he snatched a bottle of fermented algae from the side table. "At least they stopped you." He pushed past me toward the door, pausing and glaring at me over his shoulder. "I might not be able to control you, but at least that barbarian raider put you in your place and sent you away. I can thank the brute for that."

Then he staggered from the dwelling, no doubt to get drunk enough to forget the horrible things he'd said.

"Sienna." Juliette still stood with her eyes brimming with tears. "You know he didn't mean it."

I waved a hand at her. As much as I loved my little sister, I couldn't deal with her sad apologies on behalf of our father. Part of me hated her for making excuses for him almost as much as I hated him. "It doesn't matter. I'm going to bed."

I strode past her toward my bedroom.

"I'm sorry about what happened today—in the arena," she called after me. "Everyone says you were kicking ass until they discovered you were a woman."

I couldn't stop myself from smiling at this as I paused in my doorway without turning around. Mostly because she'd used the phrase "kicking ass," which she knew was a personal favorite. "Yeah, I was."

"Are you okay, Sienna?"

All my anger at her melted away, like it always did when I remembered that Juliette was so forgiving of our father because she was the kindest one of us and was so much like our mother. Even though I missed her terribly, I was nothing like our mother. Juliette had gotten all the softness, while my father and I were all rage and sharp edges.

Then I thought about Corvak and the deal he'd made with me. "I will be." I twisted my head to peer at her down the dark hall. "Can you leave me some extra pastries tomorrow?"

"Sure." She sounded happier, like she always did when she talked about her baking or even thought about it. "I know you like the ones with extra sugar."

My heart squeezed, both with affection for my sweet sister and guilt for keeping secrets from her. "Thanks, Juls."

I left her standing in the hall and closed my bedroom door behind me, grateful to finally be alone and flop down on my bed. I'd barely had time to digest the deal I'd made with the Vandar before I was facing off against my father. My heart still hadn't stopped pounding, although thinking of Corvak wasn't helping slow it down.

Had he really agreed to teach me? My gambit of sneaking into his dwelling had been a long shot. I hadn't thought it would actually work but threatening to hound him day and night had done the trick. Actually, it had been the fact that he needed something from me that had been the deciding factor.

My cheeks warmed at the thought of the payment I'd thought he was demanding and how I'd been more than willing to give it to him.

"Jeez, Sienna," I whispered as I stared up at the darkened ceiling. "Way to play hard to get."

But he hadn't wanted to bed me. He'd wanted my help in escaping from the planet. My stomach tightened into a hard ball at the idea of him leaving. Even though he said it wouldn't be soon, the thought of him leaving at all made the pit in my stomach churn.

I'd never reacted to anyone the way I reacted to him. His touch seared my skin and sent shivers racing down my spine. I wanted nothing more than to run my fingers down the hard planes of his chest and the bumpy ridges of his stomach, and then dip my fingers beneath the waistband of his leather skirt and see what other surprises the Vandar was hiding.

Heat throbbed between my legs, and I rolled over toward the wall.

"You're being an idiot, Sienna," I told myself. "He sees you as a means to an end. Nothing more. So get your head on straight and focus on him teaching you to fight."

I closed my eyes, but as much as I tried to think about anything else, the image of the bare-chested, scarred Vandar warrior looming over me—his tail swishing behind him and his dark eyes flashing—was burned into my brain as I fell asleep.

CHAPTER ELEVEN

Ch 11

Corvak

I brushed dust off my chest as I strode up the winding path toward my quarters, but the beading sweat only smeared the dirt across my muscles, making streaks on top of my markings. I didn't mind. It was right for a warrior to carry evidence of his battles, and today had been a battle.

I grunted, as I thought back to the fighters I'd drilled in the amphitheater, taking a turn facing off against each one of them so I could assess their skills. It had been a long, hot day, but by the end I could confidently say that the planet was in serious trouble. At least, if they were counting on the males I'd been given to teach.

Donal, the human I disked most of all, had enough bulk to be a decent grappler, but he had no talent and less grace. But what he didn't have in those, he made up for in brazen confidence. The Kimitherians, on the other hand, suffered from a lack of courage and a general distaste for offending anyone, even their opponent. It had made teaching them a challenge.

For the hundredth time that day, I longed to be surrounded by Vandar warriors who lived and breathed battle, and the cool darkness of our warbirds. I swept the back of my hand across my slick forehead. There was nothing cool or dark about Kimithion III—not with two suns and three moons. Even their nights were illuminated brighter than the command deck on our horde ships.

I entered my quarters, grateful for the break from the chatter of conversation that rose up from the village square. The space was furnished sparsely, but that was something I was used to from my quarters on the Vandar warbird. Actually, on the warbird I hadn't enjoyed a private kitchen or bathing chamber. Not that I'd minded eating and bathing with my fellow raiders. It was something I'd done since I was an apprentice. It was the solitude on this planet that I was unused to—taking my meals alone and not in a crowded mess, with my Vandar brothers chugging ale and laughing loudly. Yet another punishment of my exile was that I hadn't grown used to the native food, although I had visited the shops Sienna had recommended and found more familiar offerings. Still, nothing was as tasty as the bread she'd offered me.

My nose pricked as I closed the door behind me, my gaze instantly drawn to the windowsill. A wrapped bundle perched on the ledge, and the scent of yeast and sugar told me what it was before I'd even unfolded the pale fabric from around the contents.

I almost moaned out loud when I saw the collection of crusty rolls and sweet breads that Sienna had left for me. She was as good as her word, not that I was surprised. I lifted one of the twisted knots dusted with brown sugar and found something else that didn't surprise me—a folded piece of paper with a hand-drawn map and a time written in the top corner.

I glanced at the clock on the wall. It had taken me a day or so to adjust to the rudimentary method of telling time, but I now could tell from the moving sticks that I didn't have long before Sienna expected me to meet her. From the warm light slanting inside from the few windows, I knew the suns were low in the sky, and soon the moons would take their place.

Shoving the sugary bread into my mouth, I made quick work of it while I proceeded to the kitchen and chugged water from an earthenware pitcher I'd filled that morning. I would never get used to the faint brine that seemed to tinge everything on the planet. Everything except the breads that Sienna's sister baked. I ate another roll, this one without sugar, the crust crackling apart as I bit into it and the pillowy insides almost melting in my mouth. I hadn't known how ravenous I'd been, but I polished off the entire bundle of bread while I stood. When I was done, I let out a contented sigh.

The light had faded from the room, so I took the map and stepped outside again. It wasn't yet time, but I didn't count on being able to find the exact location right away. I also wanted to give myself time to go slowly enough that I could ensure I wasn't being followed or watched. Even though I'd gotten no sense that the people of the planet had been tracking me in any way, it was my instinct as a battle chief of the Vandar to be cautious to the point of paranoid.

Was, I reminded myself. I *was* a battle chief of the Vandar. Now I was stuck teaching battle strategy to fighters who could barely throw a punch.

I pushed those thoughts from my mind as I walked down from my quarters, this time, being careful to pass silently by the open windows of the other homes cut into the cliffs. The village square below me wasn't the bustling place it had been during the day. As the moons rose over the shards of mountain peaks jutting into the distant horizon and the glowing orbs were reflected in the vividly turquoise shallows, the planet's inhabitants had melted away, disappearing into their homes and closing the shops that ringed the square.

I trudged on silent feet down the stone path, skirting the edges of the square and leaving it behind. Once I'd passed the amphitheater and the path leading to the waterfront, I unfolded the map and followed the line that had been drawn. It led me behind the mountains that housed the villagers and into a scraggly forest of trees, pale bark curling off their trunks and branches fanning out only at the very top. Once I'd gone far enough into the forest that I could no longer see the beginning of it behind me, I stepped into a clearing. Although it was ringed by the forest, the ground was flat and free of trees or even trunks.

"I guessed you'd be early."

Sienna sat to one side of the clearing, perched on a log that had fallen but gotten wedged between two other trees before reaching the ground. She was dressed much as she was the day before—pants and top that hugged her body, but no cloak. That was draped beside her across the tree trunk.

"I didn't know I'd have to trek halfway across the planet," I said, folding the map and shoving it under my belt.

She laughed. "Don't tell me the Vandar warrior is tired already? Did the other fighters wear you out?"

I frowned, not wanting to admit that it had been wearing to work with pupils who were so lacking in ability. "Do you wish to learn, or do you wish to talk about my day?"

She slid off the log, wiping her hands on her pants and grinning. "Okay, tough guy. We can skip the gabbing."

I was unfamiliar with the phrase, but I was growing fond of the way she spoke. It was more colorful that the more formal Kimitherian speech, and it fit her. Although I shouldn't have been surprised, I was disappointed to see that her hair was still pulled up in a tight knot. I flashed back to imagining my fingers buried in her loose hair while my cock was buried inside her, and heat coiled in my belly. I pushed those thoughts from my mind before my cock could swell in response. I had no desire to fight with my hands in front of my crotch.

"You ready?" Sienna stood opposite me, her hands on her hips.

"I am a Vandar. I am always ready for a fight."

This made her smile. "So how do you want to start? Hand-to-hand combat again?"

I crouched into a battle stance. "Come at me, and I will deflect you."

"You mean, you'll *try* to deflect me."

Even though Sienna was confident to the point of cocky, her confidence did not bother me like Donal's did. I liked that she knew she was good. She reminded me of myself.

I returned her grin as I beckoned her forward with one hand. "We'll see, female."

She didn't run at me right away. Instead she circled me slowly, getting a bit closer each time and reversing her direction several times. Just as I was about to ask her if she'd forgotten the point of the training, she lunged at me. Ducking low to avoid my grasp, she spun around my back. It was the move she'd used on me when we'd sparred in the amphitheater, so I was ready. I whipped my tail around to grasp her by the waist as I spun to face her, jerking her flush to my body and pinning her arms to her side.

"Hey," she said as she struggled. "You used your tail!"

"Of course, I used my tail." I looked down at her. "Your opponents will use everything they have at their disposal as well. This is not a game." I released her, swatting her ass with my tail as she stumbled back. "Vandar use our tails for many things."

She pressed her lips together and nodded. "Again."

I missed the feel of her body against mine, but backed up, clearing my throat and ignoring the twitching of my tail. "If you can avoid turning your back on your opponent, you should. Keep your eyes trained on me, and watch how I telegraph my movements. Most opponents will have a tell. Look for it. Study them as you face off and plan your attack based on how *they* move, not how you do."

This information would have gone right over the heads of the fighters I'd been working with earlier in the day, but Sienna absorbed it all, her gaze tracking my feet and hands as I stalked ever closer to her. When I lunged at her, she deftly hit the ground and rolled away from me, jumping up behind me and landing a hard kick to my back.

Even though the impact stung, I turned and kept coming at her, forcing her to defend herself again and again, ducking and weaving around me, skillfully avoiding my tail when it curled too close to her.

"Good," I said, when she was breathing heavily, and strands of hair had pulled from her topknot and were flopping into her face. "Like I said yesterday, you're a natural."

Sienna reached up and pulled the rest of her hair free, and it spilled around her shoulders in a cascade of golden brown. "I'm just getting started, tough guy."

My mouth went dry, and whatever self-control I'd had started to crumble.

CHAPTER TWELVE

Ch 12

Sienna

I shook out my hair, glad to have it out of the bun. It actually hurt from being pulled up for so long, and I scraped a hand through it. Having my hair away from my face made it easier to fight, but it felt more natural to have it down. Besides, Corvak had long hair, and he managed.

The momentary pause had given me time to catch my breath, but my body tingled for more. "Ready?"

He stood staring at me for another second, then he gave his head a brusque shake. "You're skilled at keeping yourself from your opponent's grasp, but what happens when you're caught?"

"I won't get caught."

He huffed out a breath. "Confident, but not realistic. You need to know how to fight off a close-in attacker or get yourself out of a death grip."

My pulse quickened. "Death grip" didn't sound great. "You're sure this isn't some excuse for you to actually catch me?"

He cocked his head at me. "If I wanted to catch you, female, I would."

The deep rumble of his voice made me believe him and want to run. But I'd come here to learn, which meant doing things that scared me. And that definitely included being put in a death grip by a Vandar.

I straightened from my fighting stance. "Okay. Show me."

He closed the distance between us until he was so close to me I could feel the heat pulsing off his body. He took me by the shoulders and spun me around so that I was facing away from him. "You need to know what to do if you're grabbed from behind."

I sucked in a quick breath as he wrapped one arm across me from my shoulder to my hip. The iron muscles of his chest were pressed against my back, and I instinctively raised my hands to grip his roped arm.

He dropped his head so that it was beside mine as he held me motionless against his hard body. "Now what do you do?"

I fruitlessly attempted to jerk him over me, but he didn't budge. Then I tried to slip out from under his arm, but his grasp was too punishing. My heart hammered in my chest as he breathed hot in my ear.

"I'm too big for you to use leverage against me. You need to go for your opponents' weak spots."

I jerked my hips back as hard as I could, hoping to land a hit to his balls, but my ass just bumped his thighs.

He chuckled low and deep. "Not bad, but not many of your fellow fighters will be your size. And imperial soldiers wear codpieces to protect them, so your blow would not have done much good against them. Now, if you were facing me, bringing a knee up between my knees would not have been a bad idea. Vandar do not wear anything under our battle kilts."

That bit of information sent heat flooding my cheeks. Nothing? He wasn't wearing anything under those loose flaps of leather?

"Other weak spots include the instep and the eyes, if you're fighting someone who isn't wearing a helmet," he continued. "Bring your foot down hard on the inside of your opponent's—"

Before he could finish his instruction, I dropped my head and bit down on his bare arm while jamming my foot down hard on the inside of his boot. My quick succession of moves startled him enough that he loosened his grip on me. I ducked down under his arm and spun around so I faced him then I swiftly brought my knee up between his legs. At the last moment, he caught my knee in his hand, blocking it while lifting and wrapping it around his waist. His other hand curved around my back as he fell forward, taking me with him as we hit the ground with me pinned underneath him.

His hand behind my back had taken the brunt of the hit to the ground, but his entire body was pressed against me, and my leg was hitched around his waist. The impact left me gasping for breath as I attempted to push him off me.

"That was a good try," Corvak said, his face so close to mine his breath tickled my face, and I could have run my tongue down his scar.

"I can't breathe," I whispered, pressing my palms on his chest and pushing.

He lifted himself so that his body was braced on his elbows, giving me just enough space to bring my knee up again. This time, he wasn't fast enough to deflect me.

When my knee made contact, a look of surprise crossed his face then it contorted into a grimace as he rolled off me, moaning. "That was a trick."

I leapt to my feet, leaving him clutching both hands between his legs. "All's fair in love and war, right? You told me to find weak spots."

He grunted in response as he lay on the ground, doubled over in pain. My victory wasn't as sweet as I'd expected. For one, I'd injured my teacher, not an imperial soldier intent on invading my planet. And the more he moaned on the ground, the more I worried that I'd really hurt him. I didn't know all that much about males—and even less about Vandar males—but could a knee do serious damage?

"Are you okay?" I asked, stepping closer.

Another guttural groan. Great. If I'd done real damage, what was I going to do? I couldn't exactly carry the guy back to the village, and if I went for help everyone would know what we'd been doing. It would be a disaster for both of us.

I dragged a hand through my hair and glanced around. It was nighttime now, with all three moons high in the sky and the mating calls of water bugs punctuating the quiet. At least no one could hear his agonizing moans from where we were in the forest. That also meant that I was all alone in solving this problem.

I crouched down, patting his back. "Do you think you can stand?"

In response, he brought one hand up and closed it around mine, then flipped me over his back onto the ground and pinned both hands over my head as he shifted his body on top of mine.

I let out an indignant squeal. "I thought you were seriously injured. I was worried about you."

His dark eyes flashed. "Make no mistake, you did hurt me. Just not as badly as I pretended." His mouth quirked slightly. "What was the saying you used, all is fair in love and war? You tricked me, and I tricked you back."

I was very aware of how close we were, and how heavily we both were breathing. His fingers were interlocked with mine over my head as his gaze roamed my face and settled on my lips.

"I like your hair down." He lowered his head to my neck, inhaling deeply and sending an unwanted tremor of desire down my spine. "It carries the scent of sugar."

My heart was thudding so hard in my chest I was sure he could feel it echoing through his own.

"Sienna," he husked, sliding his hands down from mine and tangling them in my hair. His lips brushed my ear as he held me, and my hands went to his hair, my fingers burying themselves in his dark locks.

Need stormed through me, but also fear. This Vandar raider was so much bigger than me. He'd proven that he could take what he wanted from me, even if I fought against him. Not that I believed he would do so, but I also didn't think I would stop him if he tried. His touch was the first one that had ever provoked desire in me, and as much of a mistake as I knew it was—he had no intention of staying on my planet—I still wanted him.

He will leave you, a little voice in the back of my head reminded me. *He will leave you and never return.*

I knew what it felt like to be left, and as much as I wanted to surrender to my desire, I couldn't go through that kind of loss again.

"My sister's baking," I said as the fog of arousal cleared from my brain. "Our entire dwelling smells of it. As long as my father's fermented algae doesn't overpower it. At least my hair doesn't smell like *that.*"

His body stiffened, and then he loosed a breath and pushed himself off me. When he was standing over me, he offered me a hand up but didn't meet my eyes.

CHAPTER THIRTEEN

Ch 13

Corvak

I helped Sienna up, but my face burned with shame. I'd been so close to losing control. I'd been so close to claiming her that my cock ached, and my skin burned. I turned away so she couldn't see how my desire strained against the heavy flaps of my kilt, or how my chest heaved.

Disgust and self-loathing wracked my body, making me fist my hands by my sides. What was happening to me? A human female was the reason I was exiled. They were a weakness I'd always disdained, and one I never wished for myself. How could I desire one? How could I want one so powerfully my body trembled from the need to touch her again?

"Speaking of my sister's baking," Sienna said, her voice artificially cheery. "I snuck some rolls out with me. Are you hungry?"

I bit back the sharp retort I wished to make. None of my troubles were *this* human's fault, as much as I might want to punish her for it. The sad fact was I was stuck on Kimithion III, and she was the only human who'd proved to be at all interesting. I almost laughed at myself. Interesting was too tame a word for what I thought about her, but I also couldn't think those things about her. Not when I was planning to leave the planet and use her to do it.

When my cock had relaxed and my heart rate resumed a normal pace, I turned to her. "I've been hungry since the moment I arrived."

The smile that crossed her face was one of relief. She hurried over to the fallen log, digging around in her cloak before producing a cloth-covered bundle and waving me over to sit next to her.

When I sat next to her on the tree trunk, it settled a bit lower from my weight, and she cut her eyes to me as she passed me a crusty roll. "Let's hope we don't end up on the ground again." Then her cheeks colored, and she turned her attention to her roll, no doubt thinking about what had almost happened down on the ground.

I'd never apologized to a female before. I'd never had to. I'd also never been with an innocent one who hadn't known exactly what to expect from a Vandar warrior. Even though Sienna looked much more like a grown woman with her hair spilling around her face, she was still out of her league when it came to a Vandar raider—in every way. I was used to fighting and fucking with the same level of abandon. I was not used to tempering my desire or pulling my punches.

"Thank you," I finally said, not glancing over at her as she bit into her bread. "And I am sorry if I scared you."

Her head snapped to me. "You didn't scare me. Not that you aren't a big badass Vandar and all, but I'm not afraid of you."

"You should be." I bit into my own roll and crumbs cascaded onto my lap.

"Why? Because you're bigger than me and stronger than me and know how to kick my ass a thousand different ways?"

No, because I want to fuck you a thousand different ways.

She took a quick breath before continuing. "You might be a tough guy, Corvak, but you're not a bad guy."

I thought back to the prisoners I'd tortured in my *oblek* and even to the human female—Raas Bron's female—that I'd strapped to the wall so I could extract information from her. My life had been about fighting and death, all in the name of the Vandar cause and to free the galaxy from imperial rule, but I'd still spent years inflicting pain on others. "You don't know that."

She shrugged. "If you were a bad guy you wouldn't be sweating it out every day in the amphitheater trying to teach a bunch of clueless males how to defend their planet. You didn't *have* to teach them or me."

I'd agreed to it because I couldn't bear to leave the planet unprotected. The Vandar home world had been unprotected millennia ago, and the Zagrath had decimated it and then taken it from us. I couldn't let that happen to other planets. The people of Kimithion III didn't deserve that. Sienna didn't deserve that.

"Maybe I just enjoy fighting," I said. "There is no holo-ring on this planet, so live opponents are my only option."

She handed me another roll as soon as I finished the first. "I don't buy it."

"Buy it?" I twisted my head to look at her, stifling a grin. "You have never thought anything you haven't uttered, have you?"

She shot me a scathing look, but her own lips twitched up at the corners. "They're wrong when they say the Vandar aren't hilarious."

I enjoyed verbally sparring with this female almost as much as I enjoyed grappling with her. "Our sense of humor is underrated."

"Joke all you want, but I know the truth about you. You're a good guy buried deep underneath a grumpy, hostile warrior in a skirt."

"A skirt?" I gaped at her. "The Vandar battle kilts have been our traditional battle garb since the days when our hordes roamed the plains on our home world."

"Battle kilt? That's a fancy name for flaps of leather that look like a skirt." She eyed the kilt fanned across my legs. "I guess they are easy to fight in."

"Do not think I am overlooking you calling me grumpy," I said, swallowing the last bit of bread.

"I don't blame you for being grumpy. I'm stuck here, and I'm grumpy most of the time."

"If you are so unhappy, why have you not considered leaving?" I asked. It was clear that Sienna didn't fit in on the planet. She was too much of a rule breaker to flourish in such a controlled society.

"No one leaves."

"Because who would leave a planet that gives you immortality?" I answered my own question.

"I don't care about that," she said. "I'd rather have one lifetime filled with adventure, than a dozen lifetimes filled with nothing special. Life means more when you know it isn't forever."

"Then why stay?"

She let out a tortured breath. "My sister. I can't leave her behind with my father, and Juliette isn't like me. She likes things to be the same. She'll be perfectly happy marrying someone and having a family, spending every day doing the same thing. She says she loves the comfort of routine."

"While it chokes you?"

She turned her head to me, biting her lower lip as she nodded. "I've tried to find something I like as much as Juliette loves baking her breads. But the only thing I've found is fighting. It's the only thing that's ever made me feel alive."

"I'm surprised you were able to uncover your talent here. The planet seems so peaceful."

Her expression darkened and her shoulders bowed forward. "On the surface it's perfect, just like the surface of the shallows—placid and beautiful. But if you look under the surface there's always more. I've never been willing to accept the insults and the snide comments that were whispered or said in jest. That's why I've always gotten in trouble."

I understood this human more than I wanted to admit. "I also spent most of my childhood getting in trouble."

"Really?" She tilted her head to study me. "What do you have to do to get in trouble as a Vandar?"

"A lot." I thought of the lashings I'd received at my father's hand. "It was not until I joined a horde that I learned discipline and control."

"I never thought of a Vandar horde as disciplined. Your reputation is for swarming ships and ripping them to pieces and leaving no survivors."

"That is only partially true." My pulse quickened as I thought back to the thrill of boarding a ship, my fellow Vandar pumping fists high into the air before rushing out to cut down our enemy. "Our attack pattern might appear chaotic, but that is by design. Everything the Vandar hordes do is to keep our enemy off balance, but it is carefully planned down to the way we move as a unit, to the way our ships fly. It was my job as battle chief to coordinate all our battles and raiding missions."

"Battle chief?" She nodded. "That explains why you're so cocky."

I barked out a laugh. "We have yet to determine why *you* are."

She smiled at me—a genuine smile than reached her eyes and warmed them—then leaned back and peered up at the sky, inky blue and dotted with three iridescent orbs. "I would love to see one of your hordes."

"If it is a Vandar horde, you would not be able to see it. We use invisibility shielding to fly unseen. It is part of the reason we still evade the empire."

Her eyes shone as she swung her head down to look at me. "I can see why you miss your horde so much and want to return to it. I would feel the same way." She cleared her throat and slid off the log. "But if I'm going to help you escape, you're going to need to teach me a lot more than how to get pinned."

Too bad, I thought as I stood. Pinning her was something I would have loved to do again. If I could trust myself with her, which I did not.

CHAPTER FOURTEEN

Ch 14

Sienna

"Ow." I flinched as I bumped into a crate, almost dropping my tablet, as I counted sacks of unprocessed grain. I clutched the metal tightly, glancing at the screen to be sure it was undamaged.

My boss, a Kimitherian with a keen sense of hearing, glanced up from across the warehouse, his yellow eyes narrowing in concern from under his beige hood, although they still didn't blink. "You are bumping into things a lot today. You are sure you're well?"

"Totally fine, Krebli." I waved at him, hoping my wide grin would convince him that I was okay, even though every muscle in my body screamed out in agony. "I didn't get much sleep last night, that's all."

Krebli nodded and turned back to his own digital tablet. Lucky for me, my boss took me at my word and was more concerned with tracking the latest supplies to leave the warehouse than one klutzy employee. As long as I didn't drop my tablet. Not many places on Kimithion III used the tablets we did, but it was crucial we keep accurate track of what we imported. The tablets were another thing I was pretty good with, and I wished we had more tech on the planet.

I scooted around the grain, sighing when I realized I'd lost count and would need to start again. Why had I insisted that Corvak and I train every night? After only three evening sessions, I was already so sore I could barely sleep afterward. It didn't help my sleep that when I did doze off, my dreams were filled with Corvak, and I usually woke up sweating and panting.

Nope, I wasn't sharing *that* tidbit with my boss.

I gave my head a small shake to focus on the extremely boring task at hand. How could I count sacks of grain when my mind wanted to replay my training in my head?

Get it together, Sienna, I told myself, careful not to say the words aloud and get another concerned look from Krebli.

I might be obsessed with everything I was learning from Corvak, but I still needed this job to pay the bills. After I finally finished the grain count and tapped the numbers into my tablet, I tipped my head back and blew out a breath. The high ceiling was an arch of stone since the warehouse—like almost all the buildings on the planet—was cut into the mountain. But because it had no windows cut into it, it remained cool inside, although the various scents of grains, produce, and spices melded into a strange cacophony to which my nose had become numb. At least none of the local products from the shallows were stored inside—only what we imported from off-world. I wouldn't have been able to bear inhaling algae and seaweed all day.

"You have finished the grains?" Krebli asked as he came up behind me, his sharp Kimitherian accent making me jump.

I put a hand to my heart as I passed him my tablet for inspection. "All done. We should have more than enough until the next delivery. When will that be anyway?"

Krebli tilted his scaled head at me. "You have never cared to ask about our supply deliveries before."

I shrugged, trying to act like I didn't care. "No reason. Curiosity, I guess."

"About supplies?" He swiped a webbed finger across the surface of my tablet. "That would be a first." He nodded at the numbers I'd recorded. "Not until the moons disappear from the sky and the shallows go dark."

The natives spoke about the natural occurrences on the planet with an almost poetic reverence. "So after the new moons?"

Krebli made a clicking sound of disapproval at my simplification of the day when the cycle of the moons made them appear to vanish and their light didn't illuminate the shallows at night. But he nodded. "After that."

I felt some amount of relief. The moons were still almost fully round, which meant I had time. When I thought about Corvak leaving, my stomach clenched, but then I reminded myself that there was still time, and he couldn't go without my help.

"That is enough for today." Krebli patted my shoulder with one blue-green, scaled hand, his fingers as slender as sea kelp waving under the surface of the water. "I will see you tomorrow, Sienna."

I didn't bother to walk slowly from the warehouse, eagerly stepping outside and lifting my face to feel the warmth of the sun for a moment before flipping up my hood to keep from being burned. Since the warehouse was on the outskirts of the village, I could see the fighters trudging from the amphitheater. Their shoulders were slumped and their footsteps heavy. They looked as sore as I felt.

I hung back, hoping to get a glimpse of Corvak but he didn't emerge. Considering how quickly he moved, the Vandar was probably halfway up the mountain path to his dwelling by now. For a flicker of a moment, I considered trying to catch up with him. But then we'd be seen together, and that was the last thing either of us needed. I'd done a good job of avoiding him since we'd started meeting in secret. Even the bundles of bread I left for him were placed on his windowsill before the rest of the village was awake.

"Sienna!"

I'd been so caught up thinking about the Vandar that I hadn't heard the fast footsteps approaching behind. I stopped but didn't turn around as Donal rushed up and put himself in my path.

"Hi, Donal."

His face was red from exertion and his hair damp with sweat. Many other women considered him handsome, but I'd never been able to get past his roving gaze and arrogant smirk. "You finishing work?"

Before I could respond, he nodded. "I'm glad you've given up your attempts to be one of the fighters. It's good that you've accepted your role as a female. Not that your job is typical for a woman."

I put my hands on my hips, trying not to snap back at him even as my ire flared. "You would prefer I bake like my sister?"

He smiled at me like I was finally catching on. "Or you could fashion garments like my sisters." His gaze roamed down my body, only partially covered by my open cloak. "Although not like the ones you choose to wear."

As usual, I'd donned a pair of fitted pants and a top that clung to what slight curves I had. I couldn't move in the roomy dresses the women on my planet favored, and I certainly couldn't fight in them.

"Thanks for the input, Donal, but I'm happy with my job." I sidestepped him so I could keep walking.

He shot out a hand, grabbing my wrist and pulling me back to face him. "You won't keep it once we're married."

"Not a problem. I'm not marrying you." I jerked my hand from his grip. This guy just couldn't take a hint—or an outright rejection.

This time Donal looped an arm around my waist and tugged me back against him. "I've indulged your little game for long enough, Sienna. You *will* marry me, or you'll find your father without a job again and your sister's flour rations cut off."

Rage pulsed through me, and before I could think better of it, I'd brought my foot down hard on his instep and rammed my elbow into his gut. When he staggered back, I spun and flipped him by the arm so that he hit the ground on his back. As he lay gasping like a fish out of water, I couldn't help feeling pleased by how much better my defensive tactics had gotten.

"Sienna!" Juliette ran up to me, her hands on her cheeks. "What have you done?"

Her stunned expression brought me back to reality. The reality that I'd just beaten up a minister's son—a man who had the power to make my life miserable.

I stared at Juliette, not sure what to say. Then her face paled as her eyes shifted to something behind me.

"She was defending herself."

The burr of Corvak's voice almost made me sink to the ground in relief. I turned to see him striding toward us from the amphitheater, his expression fierce. When he reached us, he glanced down at me, his eyes searching. When he was satisfied I was unhurt, he spared a glance for Donal.

"You should not grab females from behind like that." He bent over so his head was above Donal's as the man lay flat still attempting to draw breath. "You could get hurt."

Corvak grasped his hand and jerked him to standing so hard Donal's feet caught air before coming down on the hardpacked earth.

Finally, Donal found his voice. "You should stay out of private matters, Vandar."

Corvak's eyebrows popped up, and he swiveled his gaze around us. "Private? You accosted the female out in the open. That hardly seems private."

"This doesn't concern you," Donal said, his voice vibrating with rage as he glared at me with barely contained fury. "What happens between Sienna and me is none of your concern."

"It is when you use the skills I have taught you against a female who clearly has no interest in your attentions."

Donal's cheeks were mottled an ugly patchwork of pink and red, but he drew in a breath and forced out a laugh. "You know what females are like. They say no when they mean yes."

A muscle ticked in Corvak's tight jaw, and the tip of his tail vibrated behind him. "I have never found that to be the case." He leaned in close to Donal. "But let me be clear. If I ever see you accosting the female again, she will not be the one slamming you to the ground. And when I do it, there is a good chance you will not get up."

Donal pressed his lips together and backed away, shooting a final murderous glare at me before turning and stalking off.

Juliette let out a small squeak, her hand clamped over her mouth.

Corvak's gaze tracked Donal until he disappeared into the village square, then he turned his attention to my sister. "You are the baker."

She nodded mutely, her gaze shifting between me and Corvak.

"I believe it is you I have to thank for slipping me one of your rolls the other day," he said.

Juliette dropped her hand from her mouth. "I'd just watched you drink an entire mug of algae tea. You needed it."

He bestowed a rare smile on her. "You were correct."

"You shouldn't have done that," I said to Corvak, ruining the moment. "He's a bad enemy to have."

"A Vandar does not stand by and watch a female being attacked." His dark eyes heated as they held mine. "You are sure you are unhurt?"

"I can take care of myself and fight my own battles," I said more sharply that I'd intended.

"I know you can, but battles are never won alone." He tore his hot gaze from me and bowed his head at my sister. "Thank you again."

When he walked away, we both watched him for a moment before Juliette turned to me. "What in the name of the two suns was that?"

CHAPTER FIFTEEN

Ch 15

Sienna

"Like he said, he hates bullies," I said, pushing open the door to our dwelling as Juliette followed behind me. "He saw Donal picking on me and had to step in. He's a Vandar raider. He would have done the same for anyone."

The living area was empty, and we both exhaled in relief that our father wasn't slumped over on the couch or staggering drunk around the kitchen looking for a spare change so he could buy more liquor. The scent of my sister's baking had faded, but the smell of fermented algae had not taken its place—a sure sign that our father had been gone for a while. If we were lucky, he was working. If we were unlucky, he was merely resupplying himself.

"I might be your younger sister, Sienna, but I'm not an idiot, and I'm not blind."

Nerves fluttered in my stomach. I wasn't great at hiding my feelings from Juliette. She usually knew everything about me, so it felt odd to keep something from her. "I never said you were, but I'm not sure what you think you saw."

I deposited my cloak on the back of the couch, walked into the kitchen, and poured myself a cup of water, thirsty after a long day of counting sacks and crates and eager to avoid my sister's searching gaze.

"That Vandar does not look at you the same way he looks at me or any of the other residents of the planet. He might have stepped in for anyone, but he wouldn't have looked at them like he looked at you."

My cheeks warmed at the reminder of Corvak's hot gaze, but I chugged the water and shrugged. "I didn't notice."

Juliette made a scoffing noise. "If he has some sort of crush on you, he'd better be careful. You were right about one thing. Donal and his minister father are bad enemies to have."

Now it was my turn to scoff. "I don't think tough Vandar raiders do crushes." I let the water I'd gulped down cool me off before turning and heading for the shower. They also didn't exercise caution, which was why I knew Corvak wouldn't care how powerful Donal and his father were.

My sister followed me down the short hall as I peeled off my top, tossing it through the open door to my bedroom so that it landed on the bed. I'd never been particularly modest, especially around Juliette, so I ignored her sharp intake of breath as I kicked off my pants and added those to lay beside the discarded top.

"That can't be from today," she whispered, as I edged by her in my underwear and stepped into the bathroom.

"What?" It was only when I glanced at the warped reflective surface over the wash basin that I spotted the bruises blooming across my arms and thighs. Some were fading to a sickly yellow, but others were deep purple.

Juliette's shocked expression gaped at me in the reflection. "Is this from father, or Donal, or…?" She clapped a hand over her mouth as her eyes filled with tears.

Damn. I turned and grabbed her by the shoulders. As much as I would have loved to blame my bruises on my father, or even Donal, I couldn't lie to her. And apparently, I couldn't keep my training a secret from Juliette any longer.

"It's not from either of them, I promise." I held her eyes. "If I tell you how I got them you have to swear that you won't tell anyone."

Her blue eyes became round with shock as she stared at me.

I gave her shoulders a small shake. "Promise me, Juliette. Promise me on our mother."

She went still. When we were girls, promising on our mother was the most solemn promise we could make to each other. We never said it lightly, and we never broke those promises. As she finally nodded, she allowed the hand to slip from her mouth. "I promise."

I released her and stepped back. "You remember how the Vandar kicked me from the training after he found out I was a female, and Donal made a big stink about it?"

She narrowed her eyes slightly. "Yes."

"You know I never take no for an answer. Not when I really want something. So, I made a deal with Corvak. He's been teaching me privately."

Her jaw dropped but she didn't say anything.

"I've been sneaking out at night so no one would know."

Juliette managed to close her mouth. "And all those bruises are from…?"

I shrugged. "He's training me just like he trains the males. It's hard work, and I end up on the ground a lot."

A glint flashed in her eyes. "So, that's why he was so familiar around you."

"I guess, but I promise you we're only training." I didn't want to admit that I'd touched more of the Vandar warrior than anyone on my planet would consider appropriate, or that he'd ended up on top of me with my hands pinned over my head more than a few times. If anyone knew how hot and heavy our training sessions got, they'd probably insist we marry. That thought made my stomach flutter then become a hard knot as I remembered how eager the Vandar was to get away from my planet.

Juliette absently flicked her fingers through her pale hair. "What if you get caught, Sienna?"

I sighed, reaching over and turning on the water for the shower. "We won't get caught. I've been extremely careful. We only meet after everyone is tucked away in their dwellings and fast asleep, and we go so far away that no one would ever stumble upon us. No one would even think to tramp out into the woods after dark."

My sister nibbled the corner of her thumbnail as she shook her head. "You know what would happen if someone found out, don't you?"

Actually, I didn't. There had never been an alien warrior exiled on our planet who'd been secretly training a woman in the dead of night. I could be pretty sure the ministers wouldn't be happy about it, but I suspected Corvak would face fewer consequences than I would. I flinched at the thought of our father's reaction.

I rounded on my sister. "Which is why you can't breathe a word of this to anyone. Corvak is doing this because he thinks I can help defend our planet. It would be unfair for him to get punished for it."

I didn't say that the real reason he was training me was because of our deal and my agreement to help him escape. That was something I wasn't willing to reveal to anyone, even my sister. And I didn't need to tell her that the punishment for my secret training would fall much heavier on me and even on her. My aberrant behavior would make our entire family the object of even more curious glances and whispers than we already were.

She cut her eyes to me. "Of course I won't tell anyone. I'm not a fool." She clutched my hands in hers. "But promise me you'll be careful, Sienna. Donal isn't stupid, and neither are the rest of the villagers."

I pulled my hands from hers. "What does that mean?"

She cocked her head at me and pursed her lips. "You might be clever about sneaking around, but you aren't clever enough to hide your connection. It's obvious from the way you two look at each other that you aren't the strangers you should be."

I huffed out an indignant breath as I darted a hand beneath the streaming water and determined that it was warm enough. "I told you. The only thing that's going on is battle training."

Juliette crossed her arms over her chest and eyed me, looking older than her years and so much like our mother that my heart squeezed. "That may be so, but there is something between you, whether you can admit it or not. Especially on his part."

I gaped at her, ready to argue that she was off base, but she waved a hand at me.

"You may not see it. You've never been great at noticing the way males look at you, and for some reason, you've never been aware of how pretty you are, but trust me when I say that the Vandar notices. The way he looked at you after defending you from Donal, was not the way a teacher looks at a student, Sienna."

I was not accustomed to my kid sister being the one to give me advice and watch out for me. I was also not used to her being so savvy when it came to males. "And how did he look at me, little sister?"

She turned to leave, looking back over her shoulder. "Like a predator defending his prey from other hunters."

I shook off her words, peeling away my underwear and stepping under the warm cascade of water. Corvak was training me to be a warrior. He didn't see me as his prey.

I closed my eyes, letting the water stream down my back as I thought about his dark gaze tracking me during our sessions and the dominant flash of satisfaction when he pinned me beneath him. I swallowed hard. Or did he?

CHAPTER SIXTEEN

Ch 16

Corvak

I entered the hall, finally able to pass through a doorway without bending my head and paused on the threshold as my eyes adjusted to the lower light.

"Join us!" The voice from the far end of the cavernous space beckoned me forward, the sound echoing off the arched stone walls and ceiling.

This was my first visit to the gathering hall, which was also used for the meetings of the planet's ministers. Many long tables extended the length of the hall, but only one was occupied. Fewer than a dozen humans and Kimitherians clustered at one end, all clad in light-colored cloaks, as the warm light from massive chandeliers made from bone-colored shells glowed down on them.

The cool air was a stark change from the heat outside, and I welcomed both the respite from the heat and the sunlight. I wished I'd had time to bathe before my first audience with the ministers, but the incident with Sienna and that fool Donal had distracted me and delayed my return to my dwelling.

No matter, I thought, as I strode up to where the males sat. They knew I was a Vandar warrior, and they knew I was tasked with military training. A little grime was to be expected.

The human I recognized from my first night on the planet stood as I approached. "Greetings, Corvak. Thank you for meeting with us." His gaze flitted to the dirt smeared across my bare chest. "We know you are busy with the task we gave you."

The Kimitherian who had accompanied the human Terel on that first meeting peered up at me from underneath his hood. "Are you making progress?"

I did not take a seat on the long benches with them, preferring to stand with my hands clasped behind my back as I gave my report. As I scanned the group, I wondered which minister was the father to Donal, then I forced that thought from my mind. It was better I do not know, otherwise I might have the urge to give him the same treatment I'd given his arrogant son.

I rocked back on my heels, keeping my gaze over their heads. "There has been progress. The trainees have mastered the basics of hand-to-hand combat and are learning to use weapons, although I have not found many weapons to use."

The pupil in Kerl's large yellow eyes contracted. "Since we have been a peaceful planet for so long, weapons have been unnecessary."

The concept of a culture without a means to defend itself was unthinkable to me, but I nodded as if I understood this madness. "But surely, if you believe your planet to be at risk, you should make an effort to procure some weapons. I do not wish to send my newly trained army out with rocks and spears made from sharpened sticks."

Terel cleared his throat as he worked his hands together, scanning the other males at the table. "The Vandar makes a good point. It is time we equipped ourselves with blasters."

A rumble passed through the small group and the Kimitherians' hoods shook back and forth.

I tempered my urge to raise my voice. "I am not suggesting we arm your villagers, but if you truly believe that your planet will be at risk from an imperial assault or invasion in the future, it would be wise to have a stockpile of weapons for the fighters to use. Otherwise, you will be sending them to certain death, because I assure you the Zagrath will be well-armed."

One of the other humans pinned me with a sharp look. "You do not carry a blaster."

I instinctively shifted one hand to rest on the hard iron hilt of my battle axe. "Vandar warriors are trained to use our axes as effectively as any blaster, but we are also excellent blaster marksmen. We just rarely carry the weapons on our bodies."

"Because you prefer the old ways," another Kimitherian said. "Like us."

I inclined my head at him. "In a way, yes. But our horde ships are outfitted with the latest technology—innovation even the empire does not have. We prefer to appear as our ancient ancestors, but we never reject progress. Not if it will aid in our mission or improve our chances in battle."

More grumblings.

Finally Kerl spoke again. "Even if we manage to procure weapons, they will not arrive in time."

I studied the group as they shifted on the benches. "In time for what?"

Terel let out a loud breath, shaking his head from side to side slowly. "It is probably nothing, but the empire has alerted us that a ship is inbound."

My entire body tensed. "A Zagrath ship?"

"Only one," one of the other human ministers said, his voice cracking. "It isn't unheard of for the empire to send a ship."

"There is no way they could know I am here, is there?" I asked, looking from male to male and searching for signs of deception.

"We have no open communication with the empire," Terel said. "They could not have learned it from us."

"Is *he* the reason the empire is coming?" one of the Kimitherians hissed to another, but loud enough for me to hear.

If the residents of Kimithion III did not inform the empire of my presence, I could be sure my Vandar brothers did not. Even if word had spread through the hordes, the information would not have leaked to the empire. The Vandar had no leaks. At least, we never had before.

"There is little chance that the enemy knows I am here. The Vandar would have taken great pains to keep that from them." I shot a fierce look at the Kimitherian who'd suggested otherwise, and the blue-green scales on his face turned a sickly shade of yellow. "I would bet that they are performing a scouting mission."

"What does that mean?" Kerl asked, tilting his elongated face at me.

I clenched my grip on my axe. "It means your suspicions were well-founded. The Zagrath are meticulous. Before they invade a planet, they gather information. It will appear that they are peaceful, but they will be mapping everything about your community to make their eventual incursion easier."

One of the scaled Kimitherians darted his gaze around the table. "Impossible. They haven't shown any interest in our planet for hundreds of solar rotations."

The alien made a good point. I drummed my fingers on the handle of my weapon. "Why *are* the Zagrath coming now? You mentioned that you believed they might try to invade, but what made you think that after living unnoticed for so long?"

Terel glanced quickly at one of the ministers then away again. When he met my eyes again, his cheeks were flushed. "There was an unfortunate slip. A Zagrath ship was forced to make an emergency stop on our planet not long ago. We offered the soldiers hospitality."

Realization dawned on me. Someone had let the truth of the planet's miraculous properties slip to the imperial soldiers. I studied the bowed heads and nervous twitching among the group. "One of you revealed the truth?"

All heads snapped up at once then there was vigorous shaking.

Terel expression was offended. "One of the planet's own ministers? We would never be so foolish."

His protestation of innocence was too strong for them to be blameless. "Then who are you all so eager to protect?"

Kerl straightened his shoulders and flipped back his hood. "It was the child of a minister. Someone who also should have known better but who enjoys bragging."

The human whom Terel had exchanged a nervous glance with pressed his palms flat on the table and raised himself halfway to standing. "He understands his mistake. He could not have known the imperial soldiers would take his claims so seriously."

I eyed the man, noticing a strange familiarity in the arrogant set of his mouth and the shade of his brown hair. "You are the father of Donal."

His gaze swiveled to mine, and I saw in it the same weak cruelty I'd spotted in his son. He did not acknowledge my statement, but he didn't need to.

"That is why you are so concerned and why you asked me to train your males. You didn't suspect the empire would be coming. You knew it." I slid my gaze to Terel, my blood firing as the reality hit me. "I suspect you felt fortunate when my Vandar horde reached out to you and asked you to take an exile. It was not just the financial incentive that prompted you to agree so eagerly, was it?"

The man dropped his eyes. "We thought you were the solution to all our problems."

I tightened the grip on my axe, wishing that I could swing it over my head and bring it down into the dark wood of the table. "Yet you did not tell me everything. You did not give me the information I needed."

"What do you mean?" Kerl asked.

I slammed my hands down on the table, and the males jumped back in surprise. "I have been training as if the empire *might* come, when I should have been training as if an attack was imminent. There is now no doubt in my mind that the Zagrath have targeted your planet as one of the next ones they will take over."

Terel slumped in his chair. "Then it's over."

I thumped my palms on the table again. "Not if you let me train your fighters for war, and arm your planet to fight off an invasion."

The leaders glanced at each other quickly before bobbing their heads up and down.

I straightened. "Good. That means I have a lot of work to do."

Taking long steps from the hall, I frowned. It also meant I would have little time to spare anymore. And even less room in my life for pretty distractions.

CHAPTER SEVENTEEN

Ch 17

Sienna

I paced a small circle in the middle of the open ring, tipping my head back to peer at the deep-blue sky, and the three glowing, white orbs high above. Aside from the chirping of the water crickets, the woods were quiet. No sounds of heavy footsteps tramping toward me, or even muffled ones. My cloak was draped over the fallen tree trunk, so I rubbed my arms to ward off the chill of the night.

Where was he?

After he'd disarmed me for the final time the night before, holding my body tight to his from behind as I'd tried to wiggle from his grasp, we'd agreed to the same time and same place tonight. Then I'd let him leave first, watching him stride off through the spindly trees as I'd calmed my racing heart.

I loosed an impatient breath. Did this have anything to do with what had happened with Donal earlier in the day? Shaking my head, I walked back to the log and leaned my palms against it, the curling bark succumbing to the pressure of my hands as I let my head hang between my shoulders.

I thought back, my mind scouring my memories for any indication that Corvak had been upset with me, or worried about meeting. I remembered his hot gaze holding mine but also how kind he'd been to my sister. Not anything like the gruff brute he usually was.

I stood and grabbed my cloak. Whatever the reason, it was clear he wasn't coming. I swallowed the bitter disappointment as I left the clearing, hating to admit to myself how dependent I'd become on my secret training sessions with the Vandar. Somehow, the drudgery of my job, the horrible reality of my father, and the endless monotony of life were more bearable if I knew I'd have a couple of hours grappling with Corvak.

I almost laughed. If anyone heard me say that out loud, they'd think I was crazy. Why would getting attacked, flipped through the air, and pinned to the ground be something that made my days better? It wouldn't make sense to anyone but me—and probably Corvak.

Even though he'd never said as much, the Vandar enjoyed our sessions as much as I did. It was the only time he fought an opponent with any sort of agility or skill. And when we were in full battle mode with our fists flying and our kicks high, his usually scowling expression became one of pure joy. The grumpy bastard actually grinned while he kicked my ass. He even smiled the few times I came out the victor, although he still slapped my ass with his tail.

So why bail on me? I stomped away from the trees and past the path leading to the shallows, the sound of the water bugs almost deafening now. When I reached the stone entrance to the amphitheater, I slowed my pace, hesitating at the sound of voices coming from inside. Who was there at this time of night?

My pace quickened when I realized that it might be Corvak. It didn't make much sense, but maybe the warrior decided to make a stop along the way to meet me.

I stepped into the open area and immediately realized my mistake. It wasn't Corvak. It was Donal and a couple of his friends passing a bottle of fermented algae among them as they sat on the lowest ring of stone benches. I froze and tried to back away, but it was too late.

"Sienna." Donal's voice was slurred as he leapt down and ran toward me.

I ran down the pitch-black entrance tunnel, my arms stretched out so I wouldn't hit one of the stone walls in the dark. Donal sober was bad enough. I did not want to deal with him drunk. My stomach lurched when he caught up to me and wrenched my arm back.

"I wanna talk to you." His hand squeezed my arm painfully as he backed me against the wall.

"Not now." I twisted my head so avoid the stink of algae on his breath. "You've been drinking."

"So?" He leaned his body flat against mine and the almost dead weight of him made me gasp. "You got a problem with drinking? B'cause your father's a drunk?"

My first instinct was to knee him in the balls, but I remembered what Juliette had said. Donal and his father were powerful. If I pissed them off too much it would be bad for everyone.

"I'd rather talk tomorrow." As difficult as it was, I used my sweetest and most placating voice. One I was startled to discover I had. "It's late and my sister is waiting for me."

His breath was hot on my face as he considered this. "It is late. Why are you out so late anyway?"

I opened my mouth but couldn't think of a good excuse that I could have for wandering outside the village in the middle of the night.

"You looking for me, Sienna? Is that it? You looking for me to 'pologize?"

I had no intention of apologizing since he was the one who'd been the ass, but if it would get him off me, I'd go with it. "Yep. I was looking for you. But I think it's better if we talk tomorrow."

He blew out a fishy breath that made me want to gag. "Now is better." His voice dropped to a whisper. "Now we're alone, and no one is watching."

My heart raced. He was right. Aside from his friends, who would never stand up to him, we were alone in a dark tunnel far enough away from the dwellings that no one would hear me call for help.

"My sister is nearby," I said. "She came with me so I wouldn't be alone. I really should go, or she'll come looking for me."

"Not before I show you how much I want you to be mine, Sienna." He shifted his weight, so I felt exactly what he was talking about, pressed hard between my legs. He thrust against me. "Can you feel that?"

Screw how important the guy and his father were, I thought, as anger surged within me. "I sure do. Do you feel this?" I brought my foot down hard on his instep and when he flinched and stumbled back a step, I snapped my knee up as hard as I could into his groin.

He didn't cry out. Instead, he made a high-pitched squeal before thudding to the ground.

I fumbled over his body, trying to run past him, but he grabbed for my ankle and brought me down. My knees hit the stone first and then my hands, sending pain shooting down my legs and arms.

I clearly hadn't hurt him badly enough. That, or the booze was fueling his rage and he was feeling no pain. I wasn't so lucky. My hands burned and my knees throbbed as I attempted to scramble away from him.

"No so fast," Donal said, as he tried to climb on top of me. "I wasn't done with you. I've been patient for long enough. It's time I made you mine."

"I'll never be yours," I said through gritted teeth.

"Once I ruin you, you will," he panted.

"Not if I ruin you first." I bent one leg and kicked it out as sharply as I could, hearing the satisfying crunch of bone as I made contact.

His wail of agony filled the tunnel. This time, I scrabbled to my feet and ran as fast as I could from the amphitheater, not stopping when I heard his friends' yells as they ran to his aid, or when tears of fury clouded my vision.

I barreled through the deserted village square and up the stone path. I had to get to my dwelling before Donal caught up to me.

My father was pretty useless, but even he wouldn't let Donal drag me from our front door. My legs shook, burning from the exertion of running uphill, and I was almost grateful when I rounded the corner and strong hands closed around my arms, bringing me to a standstill.

CHAPTER EIGHTEEN

Ch 18

Corvak

"Sienna?" The female heaved in ragged breaths as her body shook. Her hair was tangled around her face and tears streaked her dusty cheeks. "What happened?"

She swiped at her eyes as she looked up at me. First her expression was relieved then it darkened. She slapped at my chest. "You didn't show up!"

"I was running late," I said, glancing around the pathway at the nearby dwellings and the windows covered only by filmy curtains. I didn't tell her that I'd been running late because I'd been talking myself in and out of my deal with her most of the evening. That wouldn't calm her down, and if she persisted in shrieking, the entire village would wake up and find us together.

"Running late?" She pushed away from me, her face alight with anger. "How could you be running late? What could you possibly be doing? It's the middle of the night?"

One of the nearby curtains fluttered. *Tvek.* Before she could raise her voice again, I clamped a hand over her mouth and spun her around so that she faced away from me. I lifted her up and held her flush to my chest as I rushed back up the path and burst into my quarters.

She thrashed against me, but I jerked her to me, whispering into her ear. "I'll let you go if you promise to stop making so much noise. I don't think either one of us wants to explain what we're doing together in the middle of the night, and if you keep yelling, we'll have to."

Her body went limp against mine, and she nodded. I released her, dropping my hand from her mouth and uncoiling the arm I'd had around her waist.

Sienna spun around and slapped me, her eyes blazing. "That's for lying to me. You weren't running late, so tell me what happened."

I stared at her as my cheek stung from the impact of her hand. Instead of angering me, her blow made it even harder to resist her. Watching her chest heaving and her face flushed from rage, I wanted nothing more than to crush my mouth to hers. Which was exactly why I hadn't shown up to teach her, and what I couldn't tell her.

Even though Vandar didn't lie, I couldn't admit to her or myself that I was so weak as to desire the female I'd promised to teach. A human female, I reminded myself. The very last thing I needed or wanted. After all the trouble human women had caused me, how was it possible that one occupied my thoughts like Sienna did?

I clenched my teeth as I stared down at her, the urge to fist my hands in her wild hair almost uncontrollable. I would have to lie, as distasteful as that was to me.

"I learned something from your planet's ministers. Something that made me realize that I need to work harder to ready your people for impending war."

Sienna's mouth opened slightly. She hadn't been expecting me to say that. "What do you mean war? Kimithion III has always been a peaceful planet. We're too small and insignificant to pose any threat to the empire."

I stepped away from her and leaned my back on the nearest wall. "Your planet's effect on living creatures isn't insignificant. Immortality would give the Zagrath something that would make their empire almost invincible."

She sunk onto my stiff couch. "I don't understand. Why are we in danger now? The planet has always been like this, and it's always been a secret we kept easily."

"It's why your people don't travel off-world, or encourage interaction with other species, isn't it? And why your supply deliveries are so limited?"

The female nodded. "The Kimitherian in charge of accepting supply deliveries changes every few years, so no one making deliveries can notice that he doesn't age."

I nodded. It made sense. The Vandar awareness of Kimithion III had been limited before my horde reached out to them about accepting an exile.

"But the damage was already done," I whispered to myself.

"What damage?" Sienna asked, popping back up to her feet. "What are you talking about?"

I straightened, shaking my head. "I probably shouldn't tell you all the details, but the empire knows more about your planet than they should. They're sending a ship here, and I suspect it's a scouting mission so they can determine if the intel is accurate."

"The Zagrath are coming here?" Her flushed cheeks paled.

I grunted. "Trust me, I'm not happy about it, either. It would be a coup for an imperial soldier to locate a lone Vandar and take him prisoner. As much as I don't want to spend the rest of my life on Kimithion III, I want to spend it in a Zagrath brig even less."

She sized me up, her gaze darting around. "We should hide you. I know some spots the empire would never find, places most Kimitherians don't even know about."

I straightened and put my hands on her shoulders. "I have no intention of hiding from the empire."

"But if they find you and take you—"

I placed one finger over her rapidly moving lips. "I also have no intention of letting the empire gather information about your planet, or taking me with them."

She swatted my hand away and glared at me. "How? How are you going to stop all these things from happening? You're one Vandar and they're," she waved a hand in the air, "the empire that controls most of the galaxy."

Her voice had grown louder as she'd gotten more worked up, and I was grateful that the living quarters were built into the rock and had thick, stone walls separating them. The only drawback were the triangular windows that had no panes. The thin fabric hanging over them prevented others from peering in, but did little to muffle sound.

This time I put a finger to my own lips and stepped so close that our bodies almost touched. "Do you wish to wake the entire village?"

Her fierce expression relaxed, although her cheeks were still an alluring shade of pink. "No, of course not. But you still haven't explained how you plan to save us and yourself or what any of this has to do with you standing me up."

"I did not stand you up on purpose," I lied. "I was busy devising a battle plan and lost track of time."

Now her eyes sparked with interest. "A battle plan? Like the ones you made for the Vandar as their battle chief?"

"You remember I was battle chief?"

The pink in her cheeks deepened, and she twitched one shoulder. "Of course I remembered. I remember everything you've ever said to me."

My throat constricted as I gazed down at her. She might be a human female, but she was unlike any I'd encountered. As much as I knew an attachment to a female was a bad idea, I couldn't seem to stop myself from falling for her.

"It is too dangerous for me to continue to meet you now that the empire is coming." I rested a hand on her hip, as if holding her to me. "I do not want to risk you."

"What are you talking about? The whole reason we're meeting in secret is so I can be ready to fight by your side when the time comes."

I bit back a groan as heat prickled my skin. She was so fiery and so stubborn. A Vandar female had nothing on Sienna. "It's too dangerous. The Zagrath will not hesitate to kill a female who is fighting with me."

She lifted her chin. "I'm not afraid of the Zagrath."

"You should be." I tangled a hand in her hair and jerked her to me, tipping her head back. "You should be more frightened of a lot of things, including me."

Her breath was shallow, and her lips parted as she held my gaze, her eyes half-lidded with desire. "I've never been afraid of you. I know your bark is worse than your bite, Vandar."

My resolve crumbled, blood pounding in my ears as my tail quivered in anticipation. "That is where you are wrong, Sienna. I don't want to hurt you."

"You know I don't mind pain, Corvak." She let a breathy moan escape her lips. "I promise I can take what you give me."

I released a final desperate snarl before crushing my mouth to hers.

CHAPTER NINETEEN

Ch 19

Sienna

The impact of his kiss provoked an involuntary gasp as his lips claimed mine. I scraped my fingers up his scruff then buried my hands in his hair, partly to hold him to me and partly to keep myself from falling. There was nothing tentative about the way Corvak kissed me, his mouth dominant as it took possession of mine, but his lips were surprisingly soft. He parted my lips with a dominant swipe of his tongue, and I opened eagerly to him, moaning as his tongue stroked mine.

The hand that had braced my hip now circled to the small of my back and then moved to my ass as he ground himself into me. I lifted my knee and hooked it around his thigh, wanting to feel more of his rigid length. The tail that had been swishing behind him now caressed the inside of my leg, moving higher as I responded to his attentions.

Moving both hands to my ass, he hoisted me up without breaking the kiss and wrapped my legs around his waist. Before I knew what was happening, Corvak had pivoted and pressed me up against the wall. My legs were still wrapped around him, but he threaded his fingers with mine and pinned them over my head as he rocked his hips forward.

Even through my pants, his hard cock rubbed between my legs and sent sensations of pleasure and need arrowing through me. I pushed against his hands while squeezing my feet into his ass, leveraging the pressure to move myself up and down slightly. His deep rumble of a growl told me my movements were having the desired effect.

After a few moments, he tore his lips from mine. His dark eyes flashed dangerously as he panted. "Sienna, we can't."

I caught my own breath as my heart thundered in my chest then nipped at his bottom lip. "Oh, I'm pretty sure we can."

He rested his forehead on mine. "I can't do this to you. This is wrong."

The haze of euphoria began to clear as he released my hands and lowered my feet to the floor. I touched a finger to my swollen lips, already cooling from the absence of his warmth. "I don't get it. One second you're dry humping me against the wall, and the next you're done?"

He visibly flinched at my words, stepping back and scoring a hand through his hair. His tail no longer snapped back and forth, and his gaze wouldn't meet mine.

"This is my mistake. Not yours. I was weak. I never should have allowed myself…I never should have agreed to teach you in the first place. That was my mistake."

I shook my head, hoping to dislodge his words from my ears. "What are you talking about? You regret teaching me to fight just because we kissed? That's crazy. Who cares if we kissed? It doesn't have anything to do with you teaching me."

His eyes locked on mine. "It has everything to do with it. I knew better than to get involved with you. Even though you're a human female, and I usually despise human females, I knew it was a risk because you were different." He hesitated, his gaze softening. "You are different." Then he closed his eyes and fisted his hands. "But it doesn't matter. None of that matters." He opened his eyes, and they were cold and hard. "This cannot happen."

A chill passed through me. "Wait. What are you saying?"

He backed away from me, crossing his arms over his chest. "I am sorry, Sienna. You should go."

A sob welled up in my throat, but I forced it down. "And our fighting sessions?"

He gave a brusque shake of his head. "I can no longer teach you. I need to focus on preparing your planet to defend itself against the enemy." He held up a hand when I opened my mouth to argue. "And that is something of which you cannot be a part. You know your planet will not allow it."

"But it's a stupid rule," I said, hearing the quaver in my voice. "Especially since I'm the best fighter you have."

His jaw was tight as he looked at me, a flicker of regret crossing his face. "This was always a dream that could never be. You fighting. Us…" His words trailed off then he drew in a breath.

"We both knew that. I never intended to stay, and you cannot leave."

The truth of his words was like ice water, dousing any fire that was left inside me. The smallest part of me had hoped that after our late-night combat sessions and talks that maybe he'd warmed to the idea of staying, but it was clear his intentions hadn't changed. And my wretched life hadn't either.

In a burst of anger, I thrust my hand out hard, catching him in the solar plexus. Even though he was startled, he was only caught off guard for a second, darting his hand out and grabbing my wrist. I attempted to kick him, but he sidestepped my flailing foot, pulling me in and spinning me around so his body cocooned mine from behind.

I thrashed in his arms, but he knew all the moves I was using to get away. He knew because he'd taught them to me. After a few more failed attempts to get out of his grasp, I went still.

"I wish you'd never set foot on this planet," I hissed. "I was better off before I knew that anything better existed out there."

"I wish that, too," he husked, his breath warm on my ear as he held me tight. "More than you can know."

With a final heave, I elbowed him in the ribs and twisted from his arms, stumbling toward the door and not looking back as I ran out of his dwelling and up the rocky path toward my own. Tears made my vision blurry, but it was a route I knew all too well. It was one I'd walk up and down for the rest of my life, I thought with an ache of regret, knowing that my life would remain the same as the rotations passed, but Corvak would not be there.

"Good riddance," I muttered to myself. He might have been the most interesting thing to ever happen to Kimithion III, but he'd been nothing but a distraction for me. A distraction that had given me false hope about a life I'd never have and a reality that couldn't exist. I might not have been happy before the Vandar had arrived, but at least I hadn't been heartbroken. I'd take emptiness any day over the painful ache that now resided in my chest.

Corvak's words had been shards of glass piercing my heart. Now all that was left was a damaged shell, every punishing beat making it ache even more.

I held my breath as I slipped through the door and stumbled by my sleeping father snoring on the couch, too drunk to even notice my late arrival. When I reached my bedroom, I curled up onto the bed and pulled my knees into my chest. Even though I was alone, I refused to let anymore tears fall.

I would not cry over the Vandar raider. I clenched my fists and made myself into a tighter ball. No, I would focus all my pain and hurt on hating him instead.

CHAPTER TWENTY

Ch 20

Corvak

Tvek. The sharp pain in my neck woke me, and I bolted upright, expecting to find an attacker. But there was no one in the living area of my quarters. Early-morning light sifted through the windows and dust motes danced in the hazy beams. No unusual sounds pricked my ears, only the distant song of a bird greeting the suns.

I rubbed my neck and glanced back at the couch on which I sat. The pain had come from attempting to compress my oversized body onto a compact couch and sleeping with my neck at an unnaturally sharp angle. I grumbled as I massaged the tender spot on my neck, the pain radiating down my shoulder.

"Just what I need before a battle. The inability to turn my neck."

I cast another dark glance at the offending couch, as if it was the fault of the worn furniture, when in fact I had no one to blame for my current mood or pain but myself. I remembered Sienna running from my quarters and touched a hand to my gut where she'd landed her last blow. I almost longed for the pain of her sharp elbow, instead of the dull ache of regret that now consumed me.

After I'd watched her rush off, I had paced in front of the couch for what felt like an eternity, debating whether or not I should go after her. Even though I desperately wanted to talk to her and make her understand, I knew it was for the best if there was a clean break. Even if she despised me for it. I'd finally flopped down onto the couch and let sleep overtake me, too weary to stagger back to the sleeping chamber.

"Which was a mistake," I mumbled, as I tried to swivel my neck, flinching from the pain.

Standing, I walked to the galley kitchen, my gaze resting briefly on the empty windowsill. There were no fresh pastries wrapped up in rough cloth this morning. As much as I'd welcomed the crusty rolls and sugar-coated breads each morning, wolfing them down eagerly as crumbs cascaded from my lips and scattered onto the floor, it was Sienna's gifting of them that I missed. Knowing that the female had crept to my sill and tucked the warm bread inside the sheer curtain had given me a small thrill each morning, and made the day's tasks seem less arduous.

I shook it off, frowning at how soft I'd gotten. I'd never had breakfast delivered to me on the Vandar warbird, nor had our bread been as delicious as the creations Sienna's sister baked. Is this what happened to warriors when they were around human females for too long? Is this what happened to Kratos and Bron?

Had their minds gone soft with thoughts of the women, their bodies powerless to resist them?

I slammed a hand on the stone counter, glad for the sharp sting to snap me out of my funk. It didn't matter. I no longer had a human female to distract me and keep me from focusing on the battle ahead. I would not go the way of my former Raas' and let myself be ruled by my obsession with Sienna.

I chugged the last of the water from a nearby earthenware pitcher and strode from the kitchen, where I hooked my belt around my waist and shoved my feet into my boots. Once I'd snatched my battle axe and attached it to my belt, I stepped outside armed with my weapon and renewed purpose.

I'd done the right thing. As hard as it had been, cutting ties with Sienna had been the right move. She might be the best fighter I'd trained on the planet, but the fact remained that her planet's customs wouldn't allow it. Spending more time with her was a waste, when I should focus all my energy on preparing the villagers to defend their planet.

I stomped down the stone path, breathing in the cool morning air and grateful that the suns were still low and not yet blazing. My logical brain knew that training Sienna had been foolish, but I couldn't make myself regret it. Fighting with her, and then sitting beside her and eating more of her sister's baked goods while she told me tales about the villagers she'd grown up with, had been the best part of every day. Better than watching the graceless males in my official training class.

I forced myself to think about the humans and Kimitherians I was training. If a visit from the Zagrath was truly imminent, then I needed to step up my drills. They were not as awkward as they had been the first day, but few of them were competent enough to hold their own in a fight, and they had a difficult time moving as a unit.

I thought about moving in attack formations with my fellow Vandar warriors, our shields held high and our feet moving together in lockstep precision. After flying and fighting together for so long, we moved as one. The connectedness and feeling of being a part of a greater whole was something I'd never appreciated fully until I'd lost it. Now, being isolated on an alien planet and trying in vain to teach the concept to fighters who did not understand what it meant to be part of a tight-knit unit—a family—I missed my Vandar brethren so much I felt it in every fiber of my being.

And for the first time since I'd been exiled, I understood deeply how much I'd wronged my horde and my Raas. Staggering down the last few metrons of the path, I braced my hand on the rock ledge. In my determination to prove myself right and show the Raas that his female was deceiving him, I'd forgotten that I was an integral part of the whole. My independent actions had splintered that unit, weakening it with my need to be right. My exile had not only been a punishment for me, but it had also been a blow to the horde.

I glanced up at the sky, the pale blue already whitening as the suns rose. The Vandar were out there. As much as this planet might need me right now, I would have to return to the hordes. I was part of a greater whole, and I would not be complete unless I was joined with it. I sucked in a breath, my newfound determination giving me fresh energy. For now, I had fighters to train and a planet to defend. The Vandar never left anyone to the mercy of the empire, and I was still the fiercest of Vandar raiders.

"Corvak!" the sharp clicks of the Kimitherian voice drew my gaze across the village square.

Kerl ran toward me, his hood billowing off his face and his large eyes bugged out. The rest of the square was still quiet, only a few shop keepers opening doors and sweeping the dust off the brown paving stones, even though I detected a faint scent of freshly baked bread in the air.

I hurried forward to meet him at the obelisk, allowing the alien a moment to lean one webbed hand on the stone monument before urging him to speak.

"What is wrong?"

He thrust a cloaked arm behind him toward the shallows and the amphitheater. "It has begun."

I tried not to let my impatience brim over, but I had never been known for temperance. "What has begun?"

Were my students assembled early? Was there some sort of meeting to which I was late?

Kerl clutched my arm. "The imperial scouting ship arrived at some point in the early hours before dawn. Our planetary defenses are not powerful, especially when matched with Zagrath ships, but they also did not notify us of their approach."

I stiffened, the hairs on the back of my neck prickling. The Zagrath were here on the planet? My hand went to the hilt of my axe out of habit, and I scanned the area quickly. "How long since they landed?"

"I do not know. It cannot have been long." He glanced over his shoulder. "Since they did not request landing approval, our usual landing pad was not empty for them. They landed on the other side of the shallows, so any soldiers have a long walk to reach us."

I allowed myself a breath. That was something. A fully equipped imperial soldier with their dark uniforms and shiny helmets would trek slowly across arid land and under the heat of two suns. I placed my hand over Kerl's. "I need you to send word to all the males I've been training. I need them to assemble with me outside the village. It is time for them to put their training to use and defend their people."

He nodded, rushing past me and up the pathway to the cave dwellings. As my gaze followed him, I noticed a flash of gold hair disappearing around a bend. Although I felt a flicker of disappointment that I hadn't gotten a glimpse of Sienna, I was glad her sister was running far from the impending battle.

CHAPTER TWENTY-ONE

Ch 21

Corvak

"Is this everyone who's coming?" I stood in front of a motley group of humans and Kimitherians, most of whom appeared to still be in the process of waking.

Low mumbling told me that it was. Even Donal, who usually preferred standing in the front with his small posse of equally arrogant humans, lingered at the back of their group, his head low and a bandage of some kind over his nose.

Even though we'd spent one afternoon creating shields out of silvered wood lashed together with reeds from the shallows, the makeshift armor seemed almost comical as the fighters held them in front of their bodies. At least it was something, I thought. Since the planet didn't approve of arming its citizens, a shield was preferable to meeting the Zagrath with nothing but their dicks in their hands.

I cut my eyes to one of the warped shields trembling in a Kimitherian's grasp. Maybe not much better.

"We are not here to engage in battle with the imperial soldiers," I told the group, striding from one end to the other as my tail snapped in time to my steps. "We are gathered to make a statement."

From the terrified looks on the fighter's faces, that statement was that the residents of Kimithion III were a far cry away from being able to defend themselves. I studied the rag-tag fighting unit and considered disbanding them and meeting the enemy by myself. At least the Zagrath would not see how horribly outmatched we were.

Before I could disband them and order them to return to their quarters, a rumble of surprise rippled through the males and the villagers who'd gathered at the edge of the square. Turning on my heel, I spotted the familiar glint of the shiny black helmets.

I set my legs wide, unhooking my battle axe and holding it in one hand while the other hand rested on my hip. There were only two enemy soldiers approaching. A good sign for today, but also an indication that the empire saw Kimithion III as no threat.

When the Zagrath soldiers saw me, they both stopped.

"What are you doing here, Vandar?" one of them asked, his voice muffled underneath the helmet.

I gave them my most menacing grin. "I am a resident of Kimithion III." I tossed my axe to my other hand, catching it deftly without glancing down. "What are *you* doing here?"

The two helmeted heads turned to each other briefly before the second one spoke. "We are here to assess the need for imperial assistance."

"We have no need for imperial assistance," I said. "You may leave."

Another glance between the soldiers. "That is not for you to determine, Vandar. It is our job to assess the planet and the proper location for a garrison."

"A garrison?" I swung my axe close to the ground like a pendulum. "Why would you need a garrison of soldiers if this planet has no need of your presence?"

"As we said before, Vandar. This is not up to you. This is up to the empire."

I cocked my head at them, my heart beating in time to my swinging axe, but my tail snapping at twice the speed. "Why would the empire have any dominion over the independent planet of Kimithion III? We have no precious minerals for you to strip us bare of, or any other natural resources for which the Zagrath might need to plunder and pillage the land."

"You should not speak of the empire this way," one of the soldiers said, taking a step forward.

"Or what?" I growled. "You'll sneak a scouting ship onto the planet and build an illegal garrison of soldiers?"

The fighters behind me shifted nervously, and the Zagrath spoke in low tones to each other.

"We hoped this might be a peaceful occupation, but the empire can occupy your planet by force if need be." The soldier's voice was raised so the villagers could hear him.

I took a long stride toward them, my battle axe still swishing. "No imperial occupation is peaceful. You are leeches who suck the life from everything you touch and leave death and emptiness in your wake." I glared at them, even though I could not see their eyes behind the glossy black of the helmets. "The people of Kimithion III reject your proposal to build a garrison, and they reject your disingenuous offer of assistance. They have ruled themselves for millennia, and they will continue to do so without your malicious and greedy interference."

"We wish to speak to the leader of this planet," one of the soldiers called out. "We know this Vandar thug does not speak for the good people of Kimithion III."

My tail swept a wide path behind me as I instinctively crouched into a battle stance. "Vandar thug? I have not heard that in a very long time, you faceless automaton. But that does not bother me. What bothers me is that you were sent to spy on this planet and its inhabitants. You were tasked to gather information that will prove that there is something unique about Kimithion III, no? Information that will prove that the residents do not age or die, is that not so?"

The soldiers flinched, telling me I was correct about their mission.

"But you're too cowardly to show your face to the people you wish to enslave, aren't you?" I said. "It must be easy to hide behind that mask as you do the empire's bidding like the brainless drones you are."

"I will face you!" One of the Zagrath ripped off his helmet and threw it on the ground as the other swiveled to watch. "I'm no coward."

I observed the imperial soldier who was no more than a boy with close-cropped pale hair. Shifting my weight from one leg to the other, I spun the handle of my axe, the bright sunlight shining off the iron of the blades. "What about your friend? He won't remove his helmet on a mission of diplomacy?"

The other soldier followed suit, revealing the darker-haired Zagrath to be older, but not by much. "This should prove to you all that the Zagrath are not cowards."

"That remains to be seen," I said, grinning at them. "But now we know that you are not as clever as you should be to go up against a Vandar."

Both clean-shaven faces registered shock before I dove forward into a roll, slashing at one of their legs as I came up. The soldier collapsed to the ground, clutching his legs which were spewing blood.

"Attack!" I bellowed to my fighters, as the other imperial soldier fumbled for his blaster, his gaze transfixed on his compatriot bleeding out beside him.

Bringing my axe up, I knocked the blaster from his hand, taking the tips of his fingers with it. He screamed in agony, grasping his amputated fingers slick with in bright, red blood.

I stole a glance at my fighting unit. Instead of surging forward, they'd fanned out and splintered. Some backed away while others walked tentatively forward with their shield over their faces, so they stumbled into each other. Even Donal, who constantly bragged about his bravery, remained at the back.

Leaping to my feet, I lopped off the head of the soldier clutching his hand—much easier now that helmets didn't protect their heads—pivoting and burying the blade of my axe into the other man's chest.

Turning back to my wretched fighters, I held up my arms. "It's over."

Shields dropped and furtive gazes peered over the tops. When I glanced back at Donal to reprimand him for not joining the fight, his blackened eyes widened, and he backed away so quickly that he stumbled over his own feet.

That was when the blaster fire exploded across my shoulder. I whirled as I fell, heaving my axe in the direction of the attack and not knowing if my weapon had found its target before pain enveloped me and my world went black.

CHAPTER TWENTY-TWO

Ch 22

Sienna

I woke to a violent shaking, blinking up at my sister as she leaned over me and jostled my arm.

"Sienna!" More rough prodding of my shoulder. "You have to wake up!"

I attempted to roll away from her. If this was another drama about our father, I didn't want to hear about it. From the soft light sifting in through my window, I could tell it was still early morning. Time for her to be up due to her baking, but I still had plenty of time until I was due at work. If I went.

I flashed back to the scene with Corvak the night before and humiliation filled me, just as fresh and painful as when I'd been standing before him, and he'd rejected me. I groaned and squeezed my eyes together tighter, hoping to block out the memories and the light. Maybe I'd stay in bed all day. The last thing I wanted was to bump into *him*.

"Go away," I mumbled, flapping a hand at her and trying to get her insistent shaking to stop. "I'm sleeping."

She paused in her jostling. "You're really going to sleep through the arrival of the imperial soldiers? What happened to you wanting to learn to fight to defend our planet? Or was that all a lie?"

I rolled over to face her, sitting up so fast she nearly stumbled back. "What?"

Juliette stood beside my bed, her arms crossed and her usually placid blue eyes narrowed at me. Her cheeks were flushed from exertion, and strands of her pale hair fell into her face. "You heard me. The Zagrath ship arrived, and the fighters are assembling outside the village square."

I swung my feet over the side of the bed as I rubbed sleep from my eyes. Although I hadn't allowed myself to cry last night, my eyes still felt puffy and raw. "I don't understand. Were the Zagrath supposed to arrive so soon?"

Juliette huffed out an impatient breath. This time she sounded like me instead of our mother, and the rapid tapping of her toes as she watched me only made the similarity more disturbing.

"Am I truly like this?" I asked her.

"Like what?" Her tapping toe paused for a moment.

I fluttered a hand at her. "Do I really act this impatient when I want something?"

"Yes, you do." She grabbed my hand and tugged me to my feet. "Now are you coming, or what?"

I shook my hand from her grip. "You said the fighters are assembling right? Well, I have news for you, sister, I'm not one of those fighters." As Corvak had made abundantly clear the night before.

Juliette groaned. "Now you decide to play by the rules? I know about your secret training sessions, remember? I also know that you're an excellent fighter, so stop being a stubborn jackass and go do your thing."

I eyed her. It was odd to hear my favorite slang—and curse words--coming from my sister's lips. I also wasn't used to my baby sister being so assertive with me or anyone. The way her eyes flashed and her lips pressed together in determination gave me hope that maybe Juliette wasn't the fragile girl I always thought she was. Maybe she'd be able to make it without me someday.

"Sienna! Are you even listening to me?"

"I'm listening." I spotted my boots kicked off in two different spots on the floor and snatched them up, jamming my feet into them as I hopped toward the doorway. "But I'm not used to you yelling at me."

"Well," she said, her voice lowered, "I'm not used to imperial ships making unexpected visits to our planet. Or a Vandar leading a bunch of fighters out to meet it."

I hesitated in the doorway, shoving my last foot into the boot. "Corvak is down there? You saw him?"

She nodded, biting her lower lip. "He's the one who asked Kerl to assemble all the fighters. The Zagrath ship landed on the other side of the shallows, because it didn't get authorization to land on our landing pad."

"How do you know so much?"

She picked up her basket, which had been sitting on the floor. "Early-morning deliveries to the square."

I noticed that the cloth still billowed high above mounds of rolls I could smell from steps away. "Which you didn't make."

She shrugged. "It seemed more important to come get you and tell you what's happening."

"I don't know why." Doubt crept into my mind again, along with embarrassment about how far things had gone with Corvak before he'd sent me away. "It isn't like they'll let me join the fight."

Juliette shook her head, flipped back the cloth on her basket, and plucked out a brown, crusty roll dotted with black *carley* seeds. She shoved it into my hands as she shook her head. "Since when have you ever listened to what anyone else has said you could or couldn't do? Never," she answered for me. "Now is not the time to start worrying about what other people in the village might think. This is what you've been working for, Sienna. This is an actual fight."

I stared at the roll in my hand, warm and soft, and then at my sister with a steely glint in her eyes. She was right. I'd always wanted a way to put my talents to use, which was almost impossible on a peaceful planet that didn't allow females to fight. If there was ever a time, this was it.

For a moment, I thought about Corvak and how much I didn't want to see him, but then I brushed that aside. No way was I letting some arrogant, moody alien warrior keep me from the fight. If he wanted to go hot and cold, that was his problem. I'd trained every night for something just like this—and had the bruises to show for it—and I wasn't going to let my anger at the jerk who'd taught me ruin it.

"You're right." I took a bite of the roll, the combination of the savory yeast bread and the tang of the *carley* seeds making me almost moan out loud. I swallowed as I snagged my cloak from the hook beside the door and threw it over my shoulders. "I've gotta run."

"Be careful," she called after me with a tinge of worry in her voice, sounding much more like the sister I knew.

"You know it." I ran through the living area where my father lay crumpled under a blanket and out the door. The suns were higher now and the village square was filling up below, a reminder that I'd wasted precious time arguing with my sister.

Hurrying down the stone path, I had to push past cloaked humans and Kimitherians who were also heading down to the square. It was clear from the snatches of whispered conversation I heard as I passed that everyone already knew about the Zagrath ship. Although some people sounded curious, no one seemed frightened, which told me they had no idea why the empire was here or what it could mean to our planet.

When I got stuck behind a large cluster of old Kimitherian females, I was forced to slow my pace. Glancing over the rock ledge, I scoured the square for any signs of Corvak, my heart beating nervously at the thought of seeing him again.

You should be nervous about the imperial soldiers, not some kiss, I told myself.

But it wasn't just some kiss. It had been more than that, and it had almost been a lot more than that. Memories of Corvak grinding his cock into me had my cheeks burning, but I took another bite of my sister's roll and scooted around the old ladies, breaking into a near run as I reached the bottom of the path and heard loud voices and nervous murmurs.

A crowd had assembled in the village square, but I could tell from the raised voices that something was happening outside the village. As I tried to push my way through to the other side the loud voices became shouts and then the crowd surged back, some people turning and running for the cave dwellings.

I managed to reach the obelisk, stepping up onto the slightly raised platform. I could still only see the tops of heads, but I did spot a glimpse of Corvak's dark hair over the shorter fighters holding wooden shields. Then a shot of blaster fire tore through the air, followed by screams. More people rushed past me going away from the fight, but I ran forward—and straight into Donal.

He stared at me, his eyes ringed with purple and his nose covered in a brown bandage. For a second I thought he was going to have it out with me for kicking him in the face, but he only cast a terrifying look over his shoulder.

"They killed the Vandar," he said, before stumbling away from me and running toward the path.

My stomach lurched, but I thought he was lying. I'd just seen Corvak standing at the front. Forcing my way through the panicking crowd, I finally reached the open space where a pair of soldiers in smoke-blue uniforms lay sprawled on the ground, blood seeping into the dusty ground around them.

And in front of them, lying on his stomach as if he was sleeping, was Corvak.

CHAPTER TWENTY-THREE

Ch 23

Sienna

My knees buckled, and I fell to the ground. He couldn't be dead. He was a Vandar raider, and the toughest individual I'd ever met. It wasn't possible that he'd been killed by a stupid imperial scout. I pressed a hand to my mouth as the roll I'd so quickly eaten threatened to come back up.

Around me, people were still screaming and running but a few of the fighters with wooden shields gathered around Corvak, who lay unmoving. No blood pooled around him, but he was deathly still, and a black scorch mark covered one of his shoulders. His chest did not rise and fall, but his face was almost peaceful, his eyes closed and his scar nearly invisible. Our planet might provide long life, but it could not bring anyone back from the dead, or save them from being shot. Death, if it came in the form of an accident or violence, was still just as final.

I jerked my gaze away, unable to look upon him anymore without remembering him very alive, his heart thudding and his breath heavy as he'd pressed me against the wall the night before. I closed my eyes, forcing those memories away. It seemed almost silly that I'd been worried about being embarrassed when I saw him. Right now I'd give anything to feel embarrassment instead of the regret that threatened to swallow me whole.

I opened my eyes again, shifting my gaze to the other bodies splayed across the hardpacked dirt. The two nearest him were without helmets and one was without a head. I tasted the tang of bile in the back of my throat as I spotted a disembodied head that had rolled to one side, dirt caking the bloody neck stump. Farther away was another imperial soldier wearing his black helmet, Corvak's battle axe impaled deep in his chest as he lay face up, although to me, he was faceless.

Had he killed them all himself? Guilt gnawed at me. I should have been here sooner. I should have been fighting by his side. Maybe if I'd been with him instead of his useless fighting unit, he wouldn't be dead himself. A rumble of anger bubbled up in my chest—anger at myself for not arriving faster, and anger at the stupid rules on my planet which had deprived the Vandar of someone who would have had his back.

I pushed myself up to my feet even though my legs trembled. I needed to get away before I lost it and made a scene that I'd live to regret. Now that Corvak was gone, life would return to normal for me. No late-night training sessions. No sneaking bundles of bread onto his windowsill. No quickening of my pulse when I heard him tramp through the woods toward me.

Everything would return to the normal drudgery that had defined my life before the Vandar had arrived.

I flicked a quick glance at the dead Zagrath. Well, maybe life wouldn't be completely normal. Someone would have to answer for them, and now we had no Vandar to defend us from the empire.

Walking forward on jerky feet, I reached the helmeted soldier and stared down at him. Even in death, he clutched a blaster in his hand, the finger on the trigger. He'd been the one to shoot Corvak, I realized. He'd shot the Vandar in the back.

"Like a coward," I whispered.

After our training sessions and while we'd eaten the bread I'd snuck from my sister, Corvak had told me many tales of the horrors the empire had inflicted on other planets and especially what they'd done to the Vandar millennia ago. They were vicious cowards driven by greed and a disregard for those they deemed beneath them, which was everyone who wasn't one of the privileged Zagrath.

Even I knew that the Zagrath were also humans, but they'd been what had been referred to as the "one-percenters" when the human home world, Earth, had been all but abandoned after its resources had been stripped and it had fallen into poverty and chaos. The humans who'd been wealthy enough to escape had left and started colonies elsewhere, using their top scientists and vast wealth to increase their lifespans and improve their biology to be more resistant to the illnesses that had plagued their former planet. They'd called themselves Zagrath to distance themselves even further from the rest of us humans, who finally made it off Earth, and had been attempting to rule the galaxy ever since.

I'd heard the barely suppressed rage in Corvak's voice when he'd spoken of the atrocities he'd seen at their hand. Now I felt that same fury as I looked down at the soldier who had shot him in the back.

Bracing one foot on the soldier's chest, I gripped the long handle of the axe and jerked it up and out. Blood seeped into the coarse fabric of the imperial uniform, staining the smoky blue material and turning it black. Scarlet droplets slid off the curved blade and speckled the dirt at my feet.

The soldier was dead. There was no question about that. Somehow, Corvak had managed to throw his axe before he fell, and his aim had been perfect. I choked back a sob as tears stung the backs of my eyelids.

"Don't you dare cry," I ordered myself, clenching the handle of the axe so tight my fingers hurt. I needed to be able to see clearly to do what needed to be done. What I *had* to do.

Even though the Vandar axe was incredibly heavy, I heaved it over my head, holding it high as my arms shook from the effort. I thought about the stories Corvak had told me about the Vandar raiding missions, and the rich mythology of his people.

According to Vandar lore, Corvak should be warmly welcomed into their afterlife—Zedna, he'd called it—where he would drink and share tales of battles with the gods of old. It didn't sound so bad, if you believed that kind of thing. And right now, I needed to believe that he'd been reunited with his people. I needed to believe his death hadn't been for nothing.

"For Lokken," I whispered as I swung the battle axe through the air and took off the imperial soldier's head. The blade sliced cleanly through the man's neck and hit the ground hard, sending a hard jolt up through my arms. I watched with satisfaction as the helmet rolled away from the body, and I leaned on the axe handle to keep from collapsing to the ground again.

As Corvak would have said, it was done.

Turning, I saw that no one had witnessed my act. Everyone was gathered around Corvak's body, the whispers and excited murmurs finally reaching my ears.

"He's alive!" Terel cried, standing up from the huddled group. "The Vandar is alive!"

I held my breath, not believing his words for a moment. Then more cheers went up around Corvak, and my heart raced at the impossible news, the blood deafening in my ears. He was alive. The sob I'd been desperately holding back escaped my lips. Then the axe handle slipped from my fingers, and I joined it in sinking to the dirt.

CHAPTER TWENTY-FOUR

Ch 24

Corvak

Tvek. The last time my head had ached so much had been the day after I'd put away almost an entire bottle of Parnithian gin by myself. I lifted a sluggish hand to touch my temple, but my shoulder twinged with pain.

"He's waking."

The hushed voice made me still, blinking slowly as I opened my eyes and registered Kerl and Terel standing by my side, along with a Kimitherian male I'd never seen before. The last thing I remembered was being outside the village after I'd taken out the two imperial soldiers. Then my memories became fuzzy. What had happened, and where was I?

I swiveled my head slowly. I was in the bed chamber of my quarters, lying on the bed. My battle kilt and boots were in a small pile in the far corner, which meant I was naked under the blanket. It didn't bother me, but it was unusual, considering how little skin the people on the planet exposed.

"Our apologies, Vandar," the unfamiliar Kimitherian said, his yellow eyes appraising me with care. "It was necessary to remove your garments to treat you."

I pushed myself onto one elbow but stopped there when my head swam. "Treat me? Why did you need to treat me?"

The three males exchanged glances.

"You do not remember?" Kerl asked, tilting his scaled face at me.

I bit back the urge to shake all three males. I was not a patient Vandar, nor was I a good patient. "Tell me."

The Kimitherian I didn't know cleared his throat, which sounded much like a croak. "You were shot by a Zagrath blaster. At first, we assumed you were dead, but the shot appears to have gone wide, hitting your shoulder and not any vital organs. You were seriously injured, though, and stunned for a considerable amount of time. That is why we needed to treat you with some of our planet's healing plant compounds. Your body needed assistance to restore itself fully."

I glanced down at my bare chest. There were no scars or marks. "And am I fully restored?"

"Lerek healed you," Kerl said, bobbing his head up and down. "You have made a miraculous recovery."

The other Kimitherian touched a webbed hand to his chest, bowing his head slightly. "I am Lerek. The planet's healer. Your injuries were severe enough to summon me from my village on the other side of the planet."

I hadn't known the planet had a healer. In a place where everyone lived forever—or close to it—the concept of healers hadn't occurred to me. Then again, it sounded like there was only one, and he didn't live close, so he clearly wasn't in high demand.

Lerek let out a bubbly laugh as if reading my expression. "Yes, there is a need for a healer even on a planet such as Kimithion III. We might be immortal, but we are not invincible." He inclined his head at me. "A fact you should keep in mind the next time you go up against an imperial soldier. It might not take long for me to traverse the distance across the planet, but the next time the Zagrath's aim might be better."

I slowly pushed myself up until I was leaning against the bed's wooden headboard. "But I killed both of the imperial soldiers. Unless…"

"There was a third," Terel said. "You couldn't have known."

I stiffened. "So, there is still a Zagrath soldier on the planet?"

"No," Terel said quickly. "You managed to kill him with your weapon before you fell. From what I hear, it was quite a feat. Then we checked the imperial ship to be sure there were no more soldiers."

I had no memory of that, but my muscles uncoiled. At least they were dead.

"And then the female…" Kerl started to say, before Terel elbowed him in the side.

"We should allow you to continue to rest," Lerek said, patting my blanketed leg. "Your body is healed, but you might feel drowsy from the compounds I used. It will wear off soon enough, and I suspect sooner because of your size."

I rubbed a hand to my head. "But the Zagrath. They will not give up so easily, especially when they don't hear from their scout ship. I should help prepare—"

"You do not need to worry about that now," Terel said. "Your bravery has bought us time and —"

"It won't be enough," I said, cutting him off. "There is no way my fighting unit can defend against the empire. Not alone."

The males glanced at each other, brows furrowing. "What do you suggest?"

"There are many in the galaxy who resist the empire. Your communications system might be old, but it can send out a subspace message, can it not?"

Kerl gave a sharp nod. "It can, but the Vandar horde that brought you will be far away by now."

My heart squeezed at the truth of this. My horde—the horde I needed to make amends with—would be too far away to receive any distress call from the planet. "It is not the Vandar I'm hoping you will reach."

I gave them the information about the encrypted channel and told them what their message should say.

"*Now* you should rest," Lerek said once I'd passed on the critical information and sunk back against the pillows.

I nodded. "Only for a short while."

Then I closed my eyes as the three males left my room, the door shutting behind them. I didn't remember everything about the battle with the imperial soldiers—and I had no memory of throwing my axe at the fighter who'd shot me—but I did recall how the fighters I'd trained had splintered when I ordered an attack. They'd been too scared to join me in rushing the enemy and I'd been left to do battle by myself.

I clenched my teeth at the bitter memory. I might be able to teach the basics of fighting, but I could not teach courage. None of the fighters I'd trained had the heart of a warrior. My breath caught in my chest as I thought of Sienna.

Correction. One fighter had the heart of a Vandar warrior. The one I'd sent away, and told that she could not fight. The one who'd stormed out of my quarters.

I expelled a long breath, regret filling me. Who could blame her for being furious? She'd worked tirelessly to become a skilled warrior, but I'd dashed her hopes. Not only that, but I'd also been moments away from fucking her against the wall. My heart hammered in my chest as I recalled how tenuous my control had been as I'd kissed her, and she'd moved her body eagerly beneath mine. She'd trusted me as her teacher, and I'd failed her in every way.

My face burned with shame. These were not the actions of a Vandar. The Vandar championed the oppressed. We didn't hold them back. And by going along with the planet's backwards rules, I'd been just as bad as the rest of the males. The truth was, Sienna was the planet's best warrior, and she deserved to fight by my side. Even if she never wanted to look at me again, I needed to tell her this.

The sound of rustling fabric made me open my eyes and snap my head to the window. A booted foot was resting on the sill, then a leg appeared. When Sienna's entire body popped through the triangular opening, her head bent to fit through, I gaped at her. "What are—?"

She hurried over to me, putting a finger to my lips. "Shhh. There are still people outside your room."

I pulled her finger away from my lips, desperate to apologize. "Sienna," I whispered, "I need to—"

"Not now, you don't," she said, climbing on my bed and straddling me. "Not before I do this."

When she bent over and kissed me, her lips soft and warm as they moved hungrily against mine, I forgot every word I'd intended to say.

CHAPTER TWENTY-FIVE

Ch 25

Sienna

None of it mattered, I thought, as I lay on top of Corvak kissing him.

My anger had seemed foolish when I'd thought he was dead, and I'd forgotten it entirely when I'd discovered that he was alive. As desperate as I was to see him, I'd had to wait until the healer had done his work, slathering him with healing compounds and giving him rejuvenating tonics.

I couldn't have rushed up and thrown my arms around the Vandar when he was lying on the dirt being revived, and I couldn't even insist on being one of the ones waiting in his quarters for a progress report. I'd spotted a few of his students loitering around the door to his quarters, but I couldn't even wait with them without attracting curious stares. As far as everyone in the village knew, Corvak was nothing to me. Except he was everything.

I pulled back and gazed down at the stunned expression on his face. Then I traced one finger down the nearly invisible scar running down his cheek, the gash now no more than a razor thin pale line. "You didn't die after all."

He reached up and ran a hand through my hair, tugging my face closer to his and breathing me in, his eyes closing for a moment. "Unless I have died and this is Zedna, in which case I hope to die more often."

I smiled at him even as my eyes filled with tears. "I thought I'd never see you again. When I saw you lying there on the ground with that awful black burn mark on your shoulder, I thought…"

Corvak pulled me down and kissed me, his stubble rasping my cheek. "It takes more than a single blaster shot to kill a Vandar."

I swatted at his chest. "Cocky alien." When he flinched, I sucked in a breath. "Sorry. I forgot you're still recovering."

"I can handle *some* contact," he said, giving me a wicked grin. "But maybe we could delay the return to hand-to-hand combat practice?"

I eyed him. "I thought that was off the table anyway."

His gaze dropped. "That was a mistake."

"What was a mistake?"

He took a shuddering breath, his body trembling beneath me. "Everything I said to you. I was wrong, Sienna. I shouldn't have told you that you shouldn't fight or couldn't fight. I never should have made you feel like you aren't the best fighter on the planet. I thought I was protecting you and myself, but I was wrong."

I stared at him, shocked by the rush of words. "I didn't know Vandar apologized. I thought you guys were a 'no regrets' bunch."

"When we are as wrong as I was, we do." He lifted his gaze to meet mine.

Something swelled in my chest that felt a lot like happiness. "I accept your apology. As long as you don't regret everything."

His brow furrowed. "What words do you wish I don't regret?"

"Not your words," I said as my cheeks warmed, and nerves fluttered in my stomach. "I hope you don't regret your actions last night because I don't regret mine." I said the last few words in a rush so I wouldn't be able to stop myself.

His pupils flared, making his eyes dark pools of desire. "I regret stopping and sending you away."

I frowned, not wanting to remember how furious I'd been at him and how badly I'd wanted to hold a grudge. All of that had melted away the moment I'd thought I might lose him and felt like a hazy memory that belonged to another version of myself. The Sienna who had a chip on her shoulder and was always spoiling for a fight. Not the version of myself that was just grateful I'd have another chance with the Vandar raider.

"It's forgotten," I whispered, very aware that there were still villagers on the other side of his bedroom door. Then I rubbed a hand across the dark swirls on his chest. "I mean, not *everything* is forgotten. I don't want to forget all of it."

"No?" He cocked an eyebrow, fisting one hand in my loose hair. "What parts do you wish to remember?"

"You're an expert in battle strategy," I lowered my head until I could feather my lips across his, kissing him lightly and then nipping at his bottom lip. "Why don't you figure it out, tough guy?"

With a low growl, Corvak lifted himself slightly off the bed and flipped me onto my back, bracing his body over mine with one elbow. Even though the movement was sudden, his touch was gentle as he stroked a hand down one side of my face, dipping his head to my neck and kissing me as he whispered, "Do you think you can be quiet?"

Ripples of pleasure sizzled across my skin, and the heat of his body on top of me made me almost lightheaded with desire. "I… I think so."

His thumb traced the line of my jaw. "Good because I'd hate for all those males outside to hear me claiming you." He lifted his head slightly, so his molten gaze met mine.

I sucked in a quick breath. At least the doors were thick and not easy to hear through, but he was right. We were tempting fate. The touch of his rough hands made it difficult to concentrate, but I shuddered at the forbidden thrill. "What if someone walks in?"

"And sees me fucking you?" His gaze took on a predatory gleam. "Then they'll have to leave in a hurry. I don't share what's mine."

I was almost afraid to ask him. "And I'm…?"

"Mine," Corvak answered, capturing my mouth in a kiss that was both possessive and sensual. His body might be as hard as stone, but his lips were soft as they moved against mine, his tongue caressing deep. I lost myself in the taste of him and the warm, masculine scent that clung to his skin. Then in a breath, the kiss shifted from gentle to fierce.

Corvak growled softly as he pressed into me, the effort he was making to restrain himself obvious. His breath was ragged as his hands slid down my body and tugged at the fabric covering me. I was suddenly very aware that he wore nothing as he lay on top of me, the thin blanket he'd brought with him when he'd flipped me onto my back the only thing between us, aside from my clothes.

Memories of the night before crowded my hazy thoughts. Not the anger and humiliation that I'd been so focused on since he'd sent me away. Those were forgotten now. It was the hunger, the thrill, the pounding desire that rushed back to me. I gave in to that driving need as I fumbled along with him to rid myself of my clothes. When we'd tossed them to the floor and Corvak had ripped the blanket from between us, he paused.

Blood thundered in my ears, drowning out any noises from outside the room, but I was aware of the stutter in his breath as he gazed down at me. I'd never been especially modest, but I'd also never considered my body something to be stared at, and never in the way he now gaped at it.

"Perfect," he husked, his gaze roaming my naked body hungrily.

Although my body was already pulsing with heat, my cheeks burned even hotter. "I'm covered with bruises."

"Like a female warrior." He moved down so he could take one peaked nipple in his mouth, the warmth of his flicking tongue sending desire to throb between my legs. "*My* female warrior."

I bit down on my bottom lip to keep from crying out as he moved to the other hard peak, sucking on it until it ached, and I was writhing beneath him. His tail, which had been stroking up the inside of my thigh, dipped between my legs, making me jerk in surprise.

Corvak glanced up, grinning at me. "My tail can be used for more than restraining you."

My eyes rolled back in my head as I arched back, letting my thighs fall open for his tail. I didn't care who was outside the room anymore. All I cared about was surrendering to Corvak. For once, I was willing to give in to him and let him dominate me. I wanted it.

The furry tip stroked the length of my folds until it found my sensitive nub. When I drew in a sharp breath, Corvak shifted himself lower, closing his mouth over me as his tail pressed at my opening. A moan rose in my throat, but I bit it back, instead fisting the sheets to keep from making a sound as his tongue sucked me until my breaths were agonized pants.

Encouraged by the bucking of my hips, he increased the tempo of his tongue until my legs trembled and the pleasure made me reckless. His tail was fully inside me now, the sensation both strange and intoxicating, but I wanted more. I wanted all of him.

"Corvak," I gasped as I shattered, my body knifing up and my vision blurring.

Before my tremors had subsided, he was moving up my body, sliding his tail out and notching his cock at my slick entrance. "Sienna." His face twisted with effort as he hovered over me on his elbows. "You have never…?"

I shook my head, still dizzy from my euphoric daze.

He feathered his lips across mine. "This will hurt, but only for a bit."

I nodded, too sated to speak or to care.

He pulled me into a deep kiss as he pushed inside me slowly. I held my breath, startled that as thick as his tail had felt, his cock was definitely bigger. Twitching my hips to adjust to him, I spread my legs wider.

"*Tvek.*" Corvak tore his mouth from mine and then drove into me fully.

I buried my face in his neck, biting down to keep from screaming as he whispered words to me in Vandar. Words I couldn't understand, but which sent pleasure skimming down my spine.

CHAPTER TWENTY-SIX

Ch 26

Corvak

It took all my control to hold myself inside her and not buck wildly like I wished to do. Her tight heat gripped my cock like a vise, and her nails scoring my back and teeth on my neck did nothing to help my crumbling restraint. I'd never been known as a Vandar who could easily control his urges, and Sienna's lusty movements were making it impossible.

"*Kor misthra?*" I whispered through gritted teeth as I kept my cock buried to the hilt inside her.

"Mmmmm." Her response was only a wordless hum, but then I realized I'd been speaking to her in Vandar and not the universal tongue. It took so much focus to stay still so she could adjust to my size that I'd slipped into my native tongue.

"Are you okay, Sienna?" I asked, this time in the right language.

"More than okay," she murmured into my shoulder as she wrapped her legs around the backs of mine. "You can move if you want."

I did want, more than she could know. But still, I moved slowly at first, savoring her warmth and tightness as I drew myself out and pushed back in. It had been so long since I'd been with an untouched female, and I did not want to terrify her with my rough fucking.

When she started to shift her hips to meet my long strokes, emitting a breathy sigh each time, my control slipped from my grasp. Sliding my hands down underneath her round ass, I tipped her hips up and plunged deeper. Instead of flinching, Sienna welcomed this, thrusting up and matching my pace. Just like on the battlefield, Sienna met me stroke for stroke.

I found her mouth again, delving in and swirling my tongue with hers. Everything about Sienna, from the sweet taste of her mouth to her velvet heat made we want more. As much as I wanted to savor the moment, I could not control the savage rhythm that overtook me as my release consumed me.

The faint keening noises she made into my mouth only fired my blood further, sending me careening over the edge when her body spasmed around me, her tightness clenching around my cock again and again. I lost all ability to think, the thundering of my heart deafening me to all else as I hammered hard. When I gave a final thrust and pulsed hot inside her, her mouth swallowed my roar.

I collapsed onto the bed beside her, pulling Sienna so that she lay half on top of me. My breath came out in desperate gasps, my chest rising and falling as I attempted to steady my breathing.

"*Kor misthra?*" she whispered, her words skittering across my chest.

I lifted my head to gaze down at her. "Did you just speak to me in Vandar?"

Sienna gave me a dazed smile. "In case you forgot the universal language again."

I slapped her bare ass. "That's for insubordination."

A look of mock outrage crossed her flushed face. "Who says you're my teacher anymore?"

"You believe you have learned all there is to know?"

She swirled her fingers across the slick skin on my chest, tracing the dark marks. "Maybe not about *everything*."

A growl rose in my throat, but I didn't let it escape. There was much more I would like to teach her in bed, as well as in the battle ring. I'd never had a student so well-matched to me in every way. Not that I'd ever taken a student to bed before.

"I believe we should resume our sessions," I said. "Or possibly increase them."

She lifted one eyebrow lazily. "Which sessions?"

My cock twitched to life, heat rushing south again. Vandar did not need much rest, and it had been a long time since I'd been with a female.

I rolled her so that she was fully on top of me. "Why don't we start with these?"

Her eyes widened and she pushed herself up, so she was straddling my waist. "I know Vandar are super warriors, but you did just survive a blaster shot. Shouldn't you get some rest?"

"Your healer was very effective. Besides, I'm feeling the rejuvenating effects of the planet already."

She cut her eyes behind her where my cock was already jutting out ramrod stiff from my body. "Trust me. Those aren't the effects of the planet."

I hesitated as I grabbed her by the hips and started sliding her down my body. "Are you sore? Is this too much for you?"

Her gaze flashed hot. "Don't worry, Vandar. I can take anything you can dish out." She braced her hands on my chest. "But if I don't get back home soon, my sister might send out a search party."

From what I'd noticed, Sienna usually came and went as she pleased. "She's expecting you?"

"I told her I was coming to check on you. She's worried."

"She knows you're here?"

"Don't worry." Sienna sat up, swinging one leg over and sliding off me. "She knows about our secret training sessions, but she won't tell anyone."

"So she thinks you were coming to check on me because of our teacher-student relationship?"

She scooped her clothes off the floor and started tugging them on. "It's the truth." She gave me a wicked grin. "She just doesn't know everything you're teaching me."

I sat up and looped an arm around her waist, pulling her to me. "Then maybe we should try to fit in one more lesson before you go."

She stifled a laugh, wiggling her pants up over her hips and then squirming out of my grasp. "Maybe I should teach you something."

I narrowed my gaze at her. "What do you wish to teach me?"

She leaned over and kissed me, nipping my bottom lip as she pulled away. "The art of patience."

I grunted and huffed out a breath. "That is not one of my many skills."

"I know." She faced me with her hands on her hips. "But just think how much sweeter it will be after you've had to wait. Anticipation can be exciting." She cut her eyes to the door. "Just as exciting as having a secret affair."

I reached for her, but she danced out of my way. "And what if I don't wish to keep you secret?"

Her lips curved down for a moment. "You know what this place is like." She hoisted herself onto the windowsill. "Besides, sneaking around is what we do, right?"

Then she disappeared out the window.

CHAPTER TWENTY-SEVEN

Ch 27

Corvak

"Any word yet?" I strode into the communications hub, my gaze alighting instantly on Kerl as he stood at a dingy console. Since I'd come from the bright light outside, my eyes took a moment to adjust to the cave. Even though I'd only taken a few steps out of the blazing, mid-day suns, the cool interior made the sweat chill instantly on my skin. I rubbed my arms, my boots slapping the stone as I walked toward the alien, who had yet to turn at my approach.

The Kimitherian had his beige cloak pulled down low so that only his elongated jaw flashed greenish blue in the dimly lit room. He swiveled his eyes to me, shaking his head. "No response. You are certain the encrypted channel is being monitored?"

It had been two standard rotations since the imperial scouting ship had landed on the planet, and I'd killed the soldiers aboard it. Two rotations since I'd been shot and recovered, and almost as much time since I'd made Sienna mine. My pulse quickened as I thought about the human female who'd been sneaking into my quarters ever since. I never knew when I would return to my quarters and find her there, or if I would wake to her slipping into bed beside me.

"The ships might not be in range," I said, shaking off thoughts of Sienna before I had to concern myself with getting a throbbing erection in front of the alien elder. "They do patrol this sector, though, so we should continue to send the message."

Kerl made a strange noise in his throat, but I'd become accustomed to the unusual Kimitherian sounds. "I am more concerned by the lack of communication from the empire."

My gut clenched. Since the attack, there had been no additional scouting ships sent to the planet, and no communications regarding their missing ship and soldiers. At my urging, we'd moved the Zagrath ship from sight and disabled the tracking devices placed inside it, but that wouldn't keep the empire away forever. Especially if they were intent in their plan to establish a garrison.

"We should assume that they are coming," I told the alien. "The Zagrath never back down if they have a vested interest." And the possibility of immortality was definitely what they would consider a vested interest.

"What will we do?" Kerl turned from the console, holding his hands together in front of him so his voluminous cloak made a single unbroken sleeve that encompassed both. "Our fighters are not ready for another encounter."

They hadn't been ready for the first one, I thought. As hard as I'd drilled them, I couldn't instill a warrior's thirst for battle, or bravery in the face of danger. Especially when the planet had been peaceful for so long and didn't even allow its residents weapons. None of my trainees had been comfortable with the violence that came so naturally to me.

"If only your planet had some sort of weapons," I said, rocking back on my heels and tipping my head back to stare at the rock ceiling. Even though I'd never entered the planet's communications hub before we'd been forced to send out a message on an encrypted channel, I'd been making the long walk away from the village to the hidden cave several times a day since then. Tucked away near the planet's only official landing pad, the dank space held basic communication technology that would have been considered rudimentary for a Vandar ship. But when you were trying to hide a secret about your planet, off-world communication wasn't a big priority.

Kerl eyed me, then let out a raspy breath that echoed off the arched walls and ceiling. "Has anyone told you the story of Kimithion III?"

I folded my arms in front of my chest. "I know little about your home world."

Even as I said this, I felt a twinge of embarrassment. I'd been living on the planet for nearly two cycles of their moons, yet I knew very little about the place, or those who called it home. I only knew that the native Kimitherians like Kerl had welcomed a small group of human refugees a few hundred rotations ago and the two groups had coexisted peacefully.

He gave a single nod of his head, his unblinking yellow eyes fixed on me. "As you might know, my species is native to the planet. Our biology is uniquely adapted to the arid climate and heat of two suns. It is said we evolved from the shallows, which is why we draw so much sustenance from it now."

I nodded. I'd tasted enough of the seaweed and kelp-based food to know that the Kimitherians loved anything that came from the planet's shallow turquoise waters. Some of the dishes had grown on me, but I still craved the savory taste of grilled meat. Even the memory of a joint of meat with a brown, crackling skin made my stomach grumble.

Kerl ignored the rumble of my gut. "What you do not know is that we were not always so peaceful. Long ago, there were two tribes of Kimitherians that stretched far across the lands and occupied much more than just the village here and the cave dwellings. But the two tribes could not live in peace. There were battles over access to the shallows, and even over the best mountains to use for living."

I lifted both eyebrows. It was difficult to imagine the placid aliens even raising their voices, much less fighting. "I take it these battles did not end well?"

Kerl's scaled lips became a pale line. "They did not. Eventually, war decimated both tribes. Our population was reduced to the point of near extinction. It was only then that we realized our mistakes and resolved not to fight. Our elders instituted strict rules on behavior and aggression, and over the generations we evolved to have no aggressive instincts. The blood rage that had dominated our planet and almost destroyed our species had been eliminated."

"That does explain a lot." Like the fact that none of the males had a single fighting instinct in their bodies. "I'm assuming the humans who joined you were also given the same rules."

"They were. When we received the distress call from a ship of human refugees, we were still rebuilding our society. We'd eliminated hostility, but we had also stripped out innovation and ingenuity. We needed new energy and we also needed new skills in our community. The humans brought with them engineers and crafters and artists—things we'd lost. Together we have built a community that is thriving, yet safe."

I bristled at the word safe. In my experience, safety was an illusion. The residents of Kimithion III had believed themselves to be safe for a long time, but one slip had brought danger to their door.

"It must have been a challenge to accept a Vandar into your idyllic world," I said. "We are notorious for our aggression."

Kerl's mouth widened into a grimace. "You were needed, as was your volatile nature. We feared that we could not repel the empire without it."

"Without some kind of planetary defenses or armaments, you will not be able to ward off the Zagrath," I said, "Even with my volatile nature."

"I'd hoped our males could be trained, but I see now that there isn't time. If no one responds to our calls for help…" His words trailed off, then he straightened. "That is why I have decided to show you."

"Show me?"

Without another word, the alien spun on his heel, his cloak flapping behind him. He strode quickly across the space, stopping and glancing back at me. He flicked the long, webbed fingers of one hand at me. "Come, Vandar."

I followed him, closing the distance between us quickly with my much longer legs. Kerl shuffled around a corner I hadn't noticed before and down a tunnel. I ducked my head as the space tightened, the scent of brine making my nose twitch. Faint luminescent flecks in the stone gave off enough light that I could make out the way forward, but it felt like we were walking down. Were we heading under the shallows?

We rounded another bend and the space opened up. Kerl fumbled on the wall, flipping a switch and illuminating the soaring ceiling. Then my jaw dropped.

"What is this?" My voice was hushed as I peered up. Shelves were carved into the stone that formed the conical-shaped underground cavern, extending almost to the top. Instead of storing food or supplies, these shelves held weapons of all kinds. Even though they looked different than the imperial blasters I was familiar with, it was apparent that they were types of blasters and bazookas. In the middle of the space, a collection of land-to-air weapons were propped on stands.

"This is where we hid all evidence of our violent past." Kerl bowed his head slightly. "These are weapons forged by our ancient ancestors, but still just as deadly. This is what you'll need to take on the empire and win."

CHAPTER TWENTY-EIGHT

Ch 28

Sienna

I lay flat on the bed, trying not to wiggle and knock all the sugar off my body. Where was he? Lifting my head, I peered down at the sugary crumbs speckling my naked body. I'd thought he'd be back before nightfall, but cool air was drifting in through the windows and making my bare flesh pebble. The natural light that had poured in earlier was fading, and soon I'd be in the dark.

This was a bad idea, I thought, flopping my head back onto the pillow. What if he'd been detained talking to the village leaders? What if he didn't come back for a long time? My heart lurched. What if the elders came back to his dwelling with him?

I shook my head gently, so my body wouldn't move too much. No, there was no reason for any of the villagers to accompany him back to his dwelling. He'd been fully healed for days now, and the healer had ceased visiting to check up on him. Besides, no one would venture into the Vandar's private sleeping chamber. No one but me.

My pulse fluttered as I thought about the subsequent whirlwind since Corvak had been healed. If I wasn't working, I'd been in bed with him, and even when I had been working, I was thinking about all the things we'd done in bed. That meant more than a few inventory miscounts, and a delicious soreness between my legs.

Heat coiled in my belly as I thought about Corvak's reaction to seeing me naked on his bed, covered in the sugary coating he loved so much on my sister's pastries.

"I hope you're hungry, tough guy," I whispered, practicing the phrase once more in my most seductive voice.

Was this stupid? Being sultry didn't come naturally to me, and a big part of me felt ridiculous trying to seduce the Vandar. Especially since I didn't have to. Corvak didn't require any tricks to turn him on when I was around. A closed door seemed to be the only prerequisite for him to start tearing my clothes off.

I huffed out a breath and shifted my legs. Was some of the sugar melting? Would I be washing caramelized sugar out of places I could barely reach?

Before I could investigate further, the door opened. I held my breath, listening for voices. I was pretty sure he'd be alone, but I did not want to be wrong about this. The door thudded shut and then boots were kicked off and something heavy hit the floor. My heart tripped in my chest. If he was undressing the way he usually did, that would have been his leather belt. Even imagining the Vandar warrior undressing made me inhale sharply. Which sent a crumb straight up my nose.

For a moment, I held my breath as the sugary crumb lodged in my throat. But it was no use. I started coughing, jerking up and sending the crumbs on my body flying onto the floor.

Corvak burst into the room, throwing open the door and holding his axe in front of him as if he expected to find an armed intruder. Instead, it was me, naked and gagging, covered in bits of pastry.

He lowered his axe and stared at me, his mouth dangling. "Sienna?"

I pounded a fist on my chest as I hacked. "Surprise."

His gaze moved swiftly across my body and then to the floor that was coated in brown crackles of sugar. One eyebrow quirked up. "What are you doing?"

I finally stopped coughing, but my cheeks heated with embarrassment. So much for being a seductress. "Like I said, I was trying to surprise you."

"By disguising yourself as a pastry?"

I shot him a look as I attempted to keep from laughing. "I was supposed to be lying down when you walked in. You'd see me covered in sugar and I'd say, 'I hope you're hungry' and then…"

His eyebrows shot up so far, I feared they might disappear into his hairline. "You did this for me? To encourage me to lick you?"

My cheeks went from warm to flaming. "I thought it might be fun. I was trying to keep things interesting."

Corvak propped his axe against the wall and joined me on the bed. "You don't need to do anything to be interesting to me." He touched a hand to my shoulder, and it came away covered in sticky crumbs. "Although this is certainly interesting."

I groaned. "This is a mess. I'll get showered and help you clean it up."

When I tried to get up, he held me by the arms, pushing me back onto the bed. "I didn't say I didn't like it." He licked some of the sugar off his fingers and made a low rumbling noise. "Sweet." His gaze flared and slid down my body. "But still not as sweet as your delicious cunt."

I jolted, his words startling me and making my mouth go dry. Corvak wasn't necessarily a male of many words, but I loved it when he whispered dark and dirty ones.

"You hungry?" I asked, my voice quivering in anticipation as I attempted to salvage my sexy line.

"For you?" he growled as he leaned over me. "Always."

He bent and dragged his tongue down my neck, stopping at the hollow of my throat to suck the tender flesh. As he licked his way down my chest, he pushed his battle kilt off and it hit the stone floor. He continued his tongue's trail down my body without pausing, suckling each of my tight peaked nipples and making me writhe and moan.

Then he sat up and stood, his cock thick and long and jutting out from his body. My gaze was drawn to it, dark lines curling around the veined shaft that matched the swirls on his chest. As much as I'd seen it over the past few days, I still didn't tire of staring at it—or touching it. I sat up, reached out, and closed my hand around the base, but my fingers didn't touch. Even now, the softness of his skin was a surprise to me considering the rigidness beneath.

I eyed his cock and licked my lips. "I want a taste."

Plucking a crumb off my own arm, I placed it on the broad crown of his cock then leaned over and swirled the tip of my tongue around it and finally closed my mouth around him to suck it off. The sweetness melted in my mouth, but what I savored most was the velvety warmth of his skin.

A groan ripped from his lips, but he shook his head. "You know I love fucking your mouth, Sienna, but first, it's my turn." He flicked his gaze lower. "Spread your legs for me. I need to feel you come on my tongue."

My eyelids fluttered but I didn't release my grip on his cock.

"Now," he ordered in the same dominant voice he used on the training field, pushing me back on the bed.

A thrill shivered through me as I did what he commanded, spreading my legs wide for him and watching with wanton lust as he buried his head between them, his hot tongue scorching me as he flicked and sucked. When the furry tip of his tail circled my slick entrance, my eyes rolled back in my head.

"So much sweeter than sugar," he whispered, as he started to fuck me with his tail.

CHAPTER TWENTY-NINE

Ch 29

Sienna

As soon as my foot touched the floor, the light snapped on. I froze even though I'd already been caught. My only hope was that it was my sister behind me and not my father.

"I knew it."

My shoulders relaxed at the high-pitched whisper. I'd take a scolding by my younger sister any day over the drunken anger of my father. I pivoted off the sill completely and straightened. "I'm surprised you're up so late. Don't you need to be up soon to start baking?"

Juliette's arms were crossed over her ample chest and one foot tapped rapidly on the floor. "I'm not up late. I'm baking. That's how late *you* are."

I swallowed hard. That meant I'd spent almost the entire night with Corvak. My face warmed at the recent memory. Not that I regretted a moment of it. "Then don't let me keep you. I'll just crawl into bed and—"

"Are you delusional, Sienna?" Juliette's whisper had become a hiss as she glared at me.

I wasn't sure what she knew, or thought she knew, but the girl wasn't stupid. I didn't have to look in a mirror to guess that my hair was tousled, and my cheeks scratched from the scruff on Corvak's face.

"I know you aren't coming home looking like that because of fighting practice," she said. "And if I know, someone else will figure it out soon enough."

"Let them," I said, the night spent in Corvak's arms giving me courage. "I don't care who knows."

"Really?" She narrowed her eyes at me. "You're happy to ruin all of us just for a few nights of fun?"

I flinched at her assessment of my situation. "This is not about a few nights of fun, and who cares if we're ruined?" I threw my hands up. "This planet is too uptight anyway."

She shook her head, two fiery blotches of color appearing on her cheeks. "And you think you're going to change that? The only thing that will happen is that you'll be ruined, the Vandar will leave, and no one will ever marry either of us. It's bad enough that I have to deal with our father, but now you're making a mess of everything, too."

Guilt stabbed at me like a blade. "You're exaggerating things, Juls. I'm not making a mess of things because no one knows anything."

She shook her head. "I've seen the way you look at him. You can't hide that. Do you really want Donal to find out that you've been," She fluttered a hand at me. "Doing I don't know what with a Vandar?"

"Donal has nothing to do with this, and he has nothing to do with me. Not anymore." I flashed back to his foul breath hot on my neck and his hands groping me roughly. No matter what happened with Corvak, I could never be with Donal. I could barely look at him without wanting to break his nose again. I guess I'd been lucky he'd been too embarrassed about getting his ass kicked by a girl to say anything to his father about that night, but that didn't mean I was grateful for his cowardice.

Juliette studied me, her expression shrewd. "What do you mean? What's happened?"

I didn't want to relive the experience by telling her, so I shook my head. "Nothing. I've always said I wouldn't marry him. That hasn't changed."

Her expression told me she didn't believe me, but she loosed a heavy breath. "What hasn't changed is our fortunes. We can't spend the rest of our days living with our father, and you know we can't live on our own."

I scowled, hating the reminder that on Kimithion III females had to remain with their parents until they married. If a female chose not to marry, she couldn't live independently, even if she had a job and could support herself. The idea of living with my father for the rest of a very long life made bile rise up in the back of my throat. Still, anything was better than having to submit to Donal.

"You'll get married," I said. "Any man would be lucky to pick you, and they'd be well fed."

"And you?" Her forehead creased with worry.

I waved away her concern. "Don't worry about me, little sister. You know I can take care of myself."

"But will he take care of you?"

For a moment, I thought she was still talking about Donal. Then I realized she meant Corvak.

She continued, without waiting for my reply. "He isn't one of us, Sienna. He never has been. I know his arrival has been the most exciting thing that's ever happened on the planet, but it's not real. He's not real."

"Trust me." I fought back a laugh. "He's real."

Her frown deepened. "You're so crazy about him you've lost your perspective. The Vandar warrior never intended to stay here. This is a pit stop for him, just another planet to defend from the empire, but he won't stay. Our village will never be home for him."

Even though I knew Corvak's plan was to escape from the planet and return to his horde, I wondered how my sister knew. Was it really so obvious, as she said?

"You know I'm right," she said. "He's going to leave, and you'll have nothing. And if anyone finds out that you gave yourself to him, we'll all be shamed."

"Maybe he won't leave by himself," I snapped back. wanting to inflict some of the same pain on her that she had on me. "Maybe I'll go with him. Like you said, there'll be nothing left for me but a long, torturous existence, living with a drunk and my spinster sister."

She reared back as if she'd been slapped. "You'd leave us to go fly among the stars?"

While I'd always relished tales of space adventure, Juliette had never warmed to the idea. When I'd talked about space battles or stories of the Vandar, she'd dismissed them as dangerous and scary. My sister much preferred the familiarity of her small village and steady routine.

"I've never fit in here. You know that. I'm like Corvak. I don't belong on Kimithion III."

Her blue eyes shone with tears. "I always knew you didn't have what it took to sacrifice for others, Sienna, but I never knew you were this selfish."

"Me?" My voice rose. "You're the one who wants me to give up my entire life, and the only chance for happiness I've ever had just because you can't handle the thought of being alone."

She pressed her lips together so hard they disappeared. "I changed my mind, sister. Being alone would be better than being with a person who'd rather abandon her family for someone who wouldn't do the same for her." She leveled a finger at me. "Has he even asked you to run off with him, or are you just assuming that he thinks this is more than a fling? I'd hate to have you planning your life around someone who's just using you for a bit of fun."

With that, she turned and stormed from my room, letting the door thud closed behind her. I whirled around, my cheeks flamed and my eyes burning with tears. She was wrong about Corvak. What we had was more than a fling. Wasn't it?

I shook my head hard as I paced angrily back and forth in the compact room, trying to shake her barbed words from my brain. What had he actually promised me? Even though we'd spent every night together since the Zagrath scout ship came and he'd been shot, neither of us had ever made promises.

We'd been way too busy fucking each other's brains out to talk about the future, or if Corvak still intended to leave the planet. We hadn't even talked about what we were doing or where it was going—not that I'd cared. I'd been too swept up in my infatuation to think about anything as practical as what would happen if and when Corvak decided to leave. Would I want to go with him? Despite my anger at my sister, could I really leave her? As much as the thought of staying on Kimithion III made me cringe, the idea of leaving my younger sister alone and at the mercy of my father's drunken temper was almost unbearable.

"She'd have to come with me," I muttered under my breath. Then I almost laughed out loud.

Even if Corvak wanted me to go with him when he returned to his Vandar horde, I doubted he wanted my kid sister tagging along. Especially since the only females ever allowed on the hordes had been mates to the warlords. And there was no way in hell Juliette would ever take a Vandar warlord as a mate.

I sank onto my bed, all the happiness of the night with my Vandar lover slipping away as I realized more and more that he was going to leave me, and I was going to have to watch him go.

CHAPTER THIRTY

Ch 30

Corvak

I bent over the whetstone that I'd erected in the amphitheater, scraping the blade of my battle axe across the surface, sparks spitting. There was no point in using the open air stadium to train the planet's males anymore—at least not for hand-to-hand combat—so I'd set it up to prepare the armaments. Aside from the whetstone I'd assembled, I'd rolled the ground-to-air missile launchers into the middle of the dusty ring. Now, I needed to determine if any of the rockets in the old armory still worked.

"What's all this?" Sienna's voice was almost reverent as she walked up behind me.

I straightened, rubbing the ache in my lower back with one hand, and turned as she approached. "How did you get in here? I blocked off the entrance."

She lifted one eyebrow at me and smirked. "Did you really think that would keep me out?"

She had a point. She did sneak in everywhere. "You are not the one I was hoping to keep out, anyway." I cut my eyes to the entrance tunnel, glad that it was barricaded from all but my wily female, then closed the distance between us and wrapped an arm around her waist. "I'm glad you're here."

Her smiled faltered for a moment. "Miss me already, tough guy?" She slapped at my chest and ducked under my arm, walking toward the launchers. "You haven't told me yet what these are."

"I planned to tell you last night, but you distracted me." I came up behind her, wrapping my arms around her and pulling her into me.

A throaty laugh escaped from her throat. "I'm pretty sure you're the one who did most of the distracting."

I bent my head low, breathing in the warm skin at her neck and detecting a faint trace of sugar. My cock twitched to life at the memory of Sienna lying in my bed completely naked and covered in sugary crumbs.

She wiggled in my grasp. "Are you going to tell me, or am I going to have to torture it out of you?"

"Mmmmm. I'd like to see what kinds of torture you'd devise. I also wouldn't mind tying you up in my *oblek* and making you scream." When she gave my arm a smack, I sighed. "What I'd meant to tell you last night was that your planet has a secret store of weapons."

"What?" She rotated to face me, still in my arms. "That can't be possible. Kimithion III is completely peaceful. Maddeningly so."

"That's what the natives want you to believe. Kerl told me the planet's whole sordid past, which included a lot of bloody warfare before humans arrived. That's why weapons were banned, and no one on the planet can fight."

She frowned at me.

"Aside from you," I added quickly.

She turned back to face the launchers. "So the Kimitherians have been hiding a bunch of weapons all this time?"

"Until now, it wasn't an issue. Your society was peaceful."

"It would have been nice if they'd told you about all this before you fought off imperial soldiers by yourself and almost got killed. So now that the empire is probably going to come back with reinforcements, Kerl showed you the secret stash?"

"Yes. He believes the time has come to use force to defend Kimithion III, especially if no one answers our distress calls."

"Distress calls?" She whirled around, her eyes wide. "Is your horde returning?"

"Not my horde. They are no doubt far away by now. But there are others who patrol this sector and despise the empire. Although it is rare for a Vandar horde to fight alongside others, we have occasionally joined with the Valox resistance, and even bounty hunters."

She bit the corner of her lower lip. "Does that mean if those ships arrive, you'll leave?"

I opened my mouth to tell her that wasn't my plan, but then I stopped. That statement wouldn't be honest. If a resistance ship came to our aid, I would be sorely tempted to leave Kimithion III and join them. It would bring me one step closer to reuniting with a Vandar horde, and that was my ultimate goal. "I don't know."

She nodded curtly, turning from me and striding over to one of the surface-to-air missile stands. She dragged one hand along the tarnished metal that was mottled with iridescent shades of blue and pink.

My gut clenched as I watched her, but I tried to shake it off. Sienna had always known of my plan. She'd been the *only* one to know. "My life has never been on this planet. You know that. I was always honest with you about wishing to leave. The reason I agreed to teach you was in exchange for helping me escape."

She nodded but didn't look at me. "I know. I thought that maybe now…" Her voice cracked and her words faded.

I raked a hand through my hair. "I'm a Vandar raider. I am not built to live a regular life on a peaceful planet like Kimithion III. I was born and bred for battle. I was a battle chief of a raider horde. Fighting the empire is all I know. It's who I am."

"Can't you do that here?" She whirled to me, her hair flying as she spun. "You can stay here with me and still fight the empire."

My chest ached as I faced Sienna, her hands in tight fists by her side. The last thing I wanted to do was leave this fierce female, but I also knew that staying on the planet would make me a shell of myself. "I am meant for the skies. Once we fight off the empire, then what? I remain here waiting for a possible attack that might never come, my blade going dull as I never age, and my battle skills fading until I'm not even fit reach Zedna and spend eternity with my Vandar brethren?"

Her fists unclenched and her shoulders sagged. "I don't want that for you."

What I wanted to do was ask Sienna to come away with me, but I was afraid she would say no. She had her younger sister to look after, and she would not want to leave Juliette with her worthless father. Asking her to make a life with me in space and possibly never see her sister again was too much to ask, even though the alternative—never seeing her again—made my heart twist in agony. "You would tire of a warrior who never faced a battle and talked of nothing but raiding missions in the past. The things that drew me to you would vanish, and you would eventually wish I'd left."

She shook her head. "I would never wish that. I—"

A rumbling overhead cut off her words. We both tilted our heads up, shielding our eyes from the suns as a dark hull descended from above.

"The Zagrath," Sienna gasped.

I squinted up, recognizing the shape of the spaceship as it dropped from orbit and extended its landing gear. I pumped a hand into the air. "That is not an imperial ship."

Sienna stared at me as I grinned at the sizable cruiser landing outside the amphitheater. "Then who is it? Vandar?"

I shook my head, not even upset that it wasn't the Vandar who'd answered the call. "Our odds against the empire just got much better."

CHAPTER THIRTY-ONE

Ch 31

Corvak

I helped Sienna over the barricade blocking the entrance to the amphitheater, and we ran toward the ship. Dust kicked up as the enormous cruiser hovered over the flat space on the other side of the open air stadium, and the ground trembled at it finally landed. I braced my hands on my hips as the metal ramp slowly lowered and thudded to the dirt.

A tall, broad-shouldered male stood at the top, silhouetted against the light from within the ship. "I had to see it for myself. The battle chief for the Vandar horde defending Kimithion III."

I fought a grin as the gold-skinned alien stomped down the ramp, his dark braid swinging from side to side. "There must not have been many bounties to hunt down since I saw you on Carlogia Prime, Kush."

"There are never enough for Tori," the Dothvek muttered, as a female with a wild mane of dark curls pounded down after him.

She gripped the steel beam connecting the ramp to the ship as she peered out. "What a wasteland." She cut her gaze to Kush. "I haven't seen a place this dry since we crash landed on your wasteland of a planet."

"I did not expect you to be the ones to answer my distress calls," I admitted. "Though I am grateful you did."

"Our pilot, Caro, used to fly for the Valox resistance," Tori said. "She still monitors all their encrypted channels."

"Welcome to Kimithion III," I said, as more of the Dothveks and bounty hunter females emerged from within their cruiser. I walked forward and pulled Sienna with me, even though she looked overwhelmed by the Zevrian female with bumps curving over her eyebrows and sharp teeth that gave her a terrifying smile.

"We did not think we would see more Vandar so soon," another gold-skinned Dothvek—Tori's mate, Vrax—said, curling an arm around the Zevrian's waist.

Tori slapped at him, but her lips quirked at the corners. "We're here to kick some imperial ass, pretty boy."

"I am grateful you answered our calls," I said. "But I am the only Vandar here." I turned and nodded at Sienna. "This is Sienna, a human I've been training."

Tori eyed her. "She any good?"

"Very," I said, which prompted a twitch of Tori's upper lip and a sharp inhalation from Sienna.

A Dothvek with dark slash marks across his chest stepped forward, clutching my arm in greeting. K'alvek was the de facto leader of the bounty hunter ship, aside from his mate, a human called Danica, who was officially the captain. "Then much has changed since we last fought by your side for the fate of Carlogia Prime."

I cringed at the explanation I owed them.

"We do not need to know why you are here," Kush said, holding my eyes with his steady ones. "Only that you need assistance to fight off the empire. There are no more honorable warriors than the Vandar."

"Perhaps the Dothveks," I said.

"Very smooth." A female with flame colored hair whom I did not recognize walked down the ramp, her hands over a swollen belly. "I like this one."

Another gold-skinned alien followed behind her, his dark hair short and the markings on his chest much like those of an elaborate breastplate. "Not too much, I hope."

The female gave a wicked grin to the alien over her shoulder. "Not as much as you, babe."

"Ignore Holly." Tori rolled her eyes and flipped a pair of shiny metal sticks between her fingers. "She's pregnant and horny, like half the females on our ship. I, for one, am just glad to get a break from all the hormones in the air."

K'alvek let out an almost imperceptible sigh. "Tori is correct. There are two other females with child on board—my mate and Bexli, the Lycithian shape-shifter. They won't be joining the battle."

"Which is a fucking shame," Holly said, flipping her red curls off her shoulder. "Bexli is a badass when it comes to fighting. But she can't shift now that she's pregnant, so it isn't as cool to watch."

Kush stepped forward alongside K'alvek. "Tell us the situation, battle chief. We came to fight by your side."

"Even if there will be no one else coming to our aid, and a population that doesn't know how to fight?"

Tori flashed her pointy back teeth as she elbowed her way between the two Dothveks. "This sounds like an epic battle I don't want to miss."

"I'm glad you think so," I said, cheered by the bounty hunter's enthusiasm about an outmatched fight against a brutal empire. "The Zagrath sent a scout ship several solar cycles ago. After informing the village that they would be sending an unwanted garrison of soldiers, I killed them."

Tori chuckled low. "Yeah, you did."

"They have not responded, or sent another ship, but it is the empire. They will not go away so easily."

Kush folded his arms over his bare chest. "They are determined to take this planet?"

The question that was implied but not asked was why the empire would want a hot, sparsely populated rock like Kimithion III?

"I have good reason to believe they are convinced of its value and will make great efforts to secure it and banish the people living here."

"Sounds like the empire, all right," Holly drawled from the ramp where she still stood, her alien mate's arms wrapped around her and cradling her belly. "Does this planet have any defenses? Any planetary shields we didn't see on the way in?"

I shook my head. "None, and until very recently I was unaware they possessed any weaponry. I've since learned of an armory. But I'm still testing the ancient weapons to see if they work after so long."

K'alvek tilted his head at me. "One ship against a potential fleet of imperial ones won't last long."

"I would never ask you to fight them off from space," I said. "I believe our best strategy is to lure them closer to the planet's surface where we can target them with surface-to-air missiles."

Tori stuck the metal sticks in her hair and rubbed her hands together. "Old school. I like it."

"I might not be able to fight," Holly said, "but I can help you reengineer your weapons to get more distance."

Kush inclined his head. "She is a brilliant engineer."

"You're hired," I said. "I will show you where I have all the launchers."

"Even with missiles, some Zagrath ships may get through and land on the surface," K'alvek said. "We should ensure that the people are safely tucked away. Those that do not wish to fight."

"The ones who do wish to join the battle are welcome to fight by our side," Vrax said from behind Tori.

"We will be ready to fight." A rush of excitement flooded my chest, and my fingers buzzed with a hunger for battle. The same desire I'd always felt when I'd boarded a Vandar raiding ship with my brethren beside me and my axe in my hand. This time there would be no other Vandar, but the Dothveks and their female mates had proven their strength in battle before. It would be an honor to defeat the empire with them. And with the human female I'd made my mate. "Isn't that right, Sienna?"

But when I turned to her, she was gone.

CHAPTER THIRTY-TWO

Juliette hurried along the stone path, her stomach roiling. She pressed her fingers to her lips, hoping to keep down her breakfast as the sharp tang of bile teased the back of her throat.

She was doing this for Sienna, she told herself, as she sidestepped a Kimitherian in a beige cloak walking in the opposite direction. It was to save Sienna.

And keep her with you, a voice whispered in her head. But she shook that voice from her mind. It wasn't about that. Well, not entirely. Her older sister was being foolish and headstrong, and she couldn't see that the Vandar was using her.

Juliette's cheeks burned as she thought about how her sister had looked when she'd snuck in the night before. Her clothes had been rumpled, her hair was a mess, and she'd sported a bite mark on her neck. She couldn't imagine what sort of depravity the Vandar was into, but her sister deserved better. Sienna deserved someone who would stay with her on the planet and share a life. A real life, not some bizarre existence flying around in a battleship fighting enemies.

Even if Sienna was bored with life on Kimithion III now, that would change, Juliette assured herself. As soon as she was married and had a child, she'd settle down and abandon her fantastical notions of leaving the planet for a more exciting life.

"Once she's given up the Vandar," she muttered to herself, drawing a curious glance from a woman passing her.

When she reached the door to the dwelling, she hesitated, holding her small fist in mid-air for a beat. Once she did this, there was no going back. No matter what happened or which future she chose, her sister would consider it a betrayal.

"A betrayal she'll get over," she whispered to reassure herself as she knocked sharply on the door.

There was shuffling inside and then the door opened to reveal and bleary-eyed Donal, his nose still bandaged, but the bruises around his eyes faded from purple to a sickly shade of yellow . He blinked at her a few times. "Juliette?" He glanced behind her. "Are you here on your own?"

She nodded, drawing in a breath to bolster her courage. "Can I come in? There's something I need to tell you."

He stepped back, swaying slightly as he held the door for her, closing it once she'd stepped inside his small dwelling. Unlike females on Kimithion III, males could live alone once they'd reached the age of maturity, so Donal had his own dwelling. She scanned the space quickly, spotting dirty dishes on the table and clothes draped over the back of chairs. One that needed a serious amount of attention.

She tried to imagine Sienna here cleaning up after Donal. The thought almost made her snort out a laugh and lose her nerve, but she pushed her doubts aside.

"So what is it?" Donal rubbed a hand over his forehead and huffed out a breath along with the strong scent of fermented algae.

Juliette wrinkled her nose. Was Donal drunk? Maybe this had been a horrible mistake. She cut her eyes to the door.

"Is it Sienna?" Donal asked, his voice sharp with concern. "Is she okay?"

Juliette released a sigh. No, she was right to do this. It was Donal who truly cared about her sister. It was Donal who could provide a future on the planet for Sienna.

"She's okay, but there's something you should know."

Creases formed along his brow as he stared at her.

"She's seeing the Vandar. She sneaks out to be with him. It's been going on for a while. At first, he was just teaching her to fight, but now it's more. I think they're…" The words which had spilled from her in such a rush trailed off as Donal's perplexed expression darkened.

"Are you telling me that this alien brute has been fucking my fiancée?"

I shrunk from him as his voice became a bellow. No way was I going to say what Sienna would—that she wasn't his fiancée. He was too livid to listen to reason.

"I don't know," I said. "I can't say for sure. I thought maybe you could talk some sense into her, or make her see how much better off she'd be with you."

He raked a hand through his hair, leaving red gashes on his temple. "Ever since that barbarian arrived, she's been different. Wanting to learn how to fight, pushing me away." He pointed to his nose. "Did you know she did this to me?"

Juliette recoiled. Sienna hadn't mentioned hitting Donal.

"She thinks she can reject me, but turn around and spread her legs for him?" He strode back and forth inside the room, bumping into a low table and kicking it hard. One of the legs shattered, and the table crashed to the floor.

Juliette slapped a hand over her mouth to keep from screaming. She hadn't expected Donal to get so angry. To her, he'd always been easygoing and friendly. She'd never seen this side of him. Had Sienna? Was that why she'd refused Donal?

Then the man turned toward her and squared his shoulders. "Don't worry. You were right to tell me."

She eyed his calm expression. "I was?"

He nodded, taking her by the elbow and leading her to the door. "I'll talk to Sienna like you suggested. I'll make her see reason."

Juliette almost sagged with relief. "You're not angry with her? You wouldn't…hurt her?"

He looked taken aback. "I could never hurt my future wife." He opened the door and propelled her out of it. "Sienna and I have always been meant to be together. She just needs a reminder."

When the door closed, Juliette stood outside, heaving in breaths. That hadn't gone so bad after all. Sienna might not be thrilled she'd gone behind her back and gotten Donal involved, but it would all be forgotten once the Vandar left, and life returned to normal. A rumble in the sky made her look up, as a massive spaceship descended from above.

For Juliette, normal couldn't come fast enough.

CHAPTER THIRTY-THREE

Ch 33

Sienna

I ducked into one of the markets off the main square, flattening myself against the cool stone wall.

"Are you all right?" The Kimitherian shop clerk eyed me from behind a table displaying a variety of glossy ceramic bowls and plates.

My heart pounded, but not from fear. I hadn't been afraid of the spaceship, and the gold-skinned aliens and females who'd emerged. They seemed perfectly nice—fun even. It was their presence and Corvak's obvious relief at seeing them that had made me panic.

The Vandar raider had spoken to them like old friends. There was none of the reticence and gruffness that he'd shown when he'd arrived here.

Because he doesn't fit in here, I reminded myself. Juliette was right. He wasn't one of us and he never would be. Kimithion III wasn't his home. He belonged in the skies with other warriors like the bounty hunters who'd arrived to lend aid. And now that they were here, Corvak would probably leave with them.

And leave me behind.

My eyes stung with tears I refused to let fall. He was casting me aside already. Although he'd introduced me at first, I'd been quickly forgotten as more people emerged from the ship and they started to discuss the empire. Corvak had seamlessly slipped into warrior mode with the other bare-chested aliens, and hadn't even glanced back at me once. It hadn't been hard to slip away unnoticed.

It was better this way, I told myself. He needed to focus on the coming battle, and I needed to get used to the idea that our fun fling was coming to an end. I bit my lip, hating to admit that my kid sister had been right about everything. Corvak had never had any intention of staying with me, or even taking me with him when he left. I'd always been a means to an end to him, the end being his escape from the planet.

"He was always honest with you," I muttered to myself, ignoring the sidelong glance from the store clerk who probably didn't want a female loitering in his shop and talking to herself. "He never lied about wanting to leave."

I couldn't blame the Vandar for his part in the ache that gripped my heart, but I could regret mine. Like always, I'd been too impulsive. I'd barreled forward into the fire without thinking of the consequences, and I'd gotten burned. I never should have allowed myself to fall for an alien who was always destined to fly away from me.

I glanced out the open arched door. Villagers were bustling through the square toward the newly arrived ship, excited murmurs buzzing through the crowd like a swarm of sea bees. The arrival of the bounty hunters in their massive ship was big news for our planet, and everyone wanted to see the impressive vessel. I almost laughed as I thought about the reactions they'd have to more brawny, shirtless males. Even though these Dothvek warriors wore leather pants instead of kilts, they also had black marks on their skin and long hair. A far cry from the iridescent blue-green scales of the natives or the unmarked skin of the humans on Kimithion III.

A pang of longing stabbed at me. I wanted to be with Corvak and his bounty hunter friends. The female called Tori looked like an especially fierce female warrior I could learn from. Besides, the battle with the Zagrath was exactly what I'd been training for, but the more time I spent with the Vandar battle chief, the more painful it would be when he left me.

I'd have to help the fight in some other way because fighting by Corvak's side would only be a torment. A taste of what life could be like with a warrior—a life I would never have.

I made my way from the shop, turning away from the ship and pushing through the flow of villagers curious to see the newcomers to the planet. Keeping my head down, I weaved my way toward the path to the cave dwellings, hoping that Corvak wouldn't come after me, but also praying that he would.

"Sienna!"

I stiffened when I heard the voice. Donal was the last person I wished to see now. Without turning toward the sound of his voice, I shook my head. "I can't talk now."

He managed to elbow his way through the crowd and step in front of me. He held his hands up as in surrender. "I know you're mad at me. I get it."

I stared at the fading bruises around his eyes and his swollen nose, a bandage still over the bridge. "Do you even remember what you did?"

He dropped his gaze to the ground. "Not really. Listen, Sienna, I was really drunk and upset, and I acted like an idiot."

Trying to force himself on me was more than acting like an idiot, but I wasn't in the mood for an argument. I didn't care about fighting with Donal anymore. It wasn't like I'd ever change him, or even cared to. Even if I wouldn't end up with Corvak, I was certain about one thing. A man like Donal who ran from fights and thought it was okay to assault females was never going to be a part of my future.

I didn't meet his eyes. "Okay. What do you want me to say?"

He reached for my hand, but I jerked it away. "I want you to say that you don't hate me."

The whine in his voice made me want to hit him again, but I reminded myself that we were in public. Besides, I didn't hate Donal. I didn't feel enough for him to hate him. I let out a weary sigh. "I don't hate you."

I started walking up the path, the number of people thinning out as I got higher. Donal followed me, almost jogging to keep up with my brisk pace.

"You don't know how much it means to me that you said that." He gave a nervous laugh. "We've known each other too long for there to be bad blood between us, don't you think?"

"Sure." Whatever would shut him up.

"It's funny that you can know someone for so long, and still not know so much about them, don't you think?"

I didn't glance over to him as he hurried along by my side. There were no more people rushing down the path heading to the village. The path and the dwellings cut into the mountain were unusually quiet, with no voices drifting from the windows and no approaching footsteps tapping in the distance. I suspected everyone was gathered around the alien ship.

My gut clenched, and my gait slowed. Which was where I should be. I stopped and gazed up the deserted path. What was I doing running from a fight? That wasn't me. Turning, I peered over the stone ledge to the empty village square, and squinted to see the stream of people moving toward the hulking gray ship.

My pulse quickened. Corvak was there, along with the other fighters who would defend the planet. As much as it pained me, I should be there, too. I'd been a fool to run from him. Warriors didn't run away when things got tough. As tough as it would be to fight alongside Corvak knowing that victory would mean he would leave, I had to do it.

"Don't you think, Sienna?"

I hadn't been listening to Donal ramble on, but now I focused my gaze on him. "I'm sorry. What?"

His eyes were intense as he stared at me, flinching slightly at my question. "I said that even after all this time, there are things I don't know about you. Like the fact that you've been fucking that barbarian." His lips curled into a sneer. "I didn't know that tidbit until your sister told me."

My skin went cold. "Juliette told you that—?"

"That my fiancée has been spreading her legs for a Vandar," he cut me off, spitting out each of his words like they were poison.

The cold prickles on my flesh became fiery. "I don't know what my sister told you, but let's get one thing straight." I jabbed a finger at him. "You are not my fiancé. You are nothing to me, and you never will be."

Anger twisted his face, his bruises and swollen nose making him look even more like a monster. His gaze flicked over my shoulder briefly and then strong hands were grabbing me from behind. "We can fix that."

Before I could jab my foot behind me or throw an elbow, pain exploded across my head. As the menacing face of Donal grew smaller, darkness swallowed me.

CHAPTER THIRTY-FOUR

Ch 34

Corvak

"That should do it." Holly blew a strand of fiery-red hair out of her face as she patted the last of the missile launchers. "I refitted them so they can blast anything out of the atmosphere, *and* I improved their homing technology."

Kush passed an armful of torpedo casings to me. "I told you she was an excellent engineer."

I eyed the female in brightly colored clothing. "I have been learning that human females are more capable than they appear."

"You got that right, Skirts." Tori lowered a pair of heavy Kimitherian guns to the ground and stood, swiping the back of her hand across the warm-brown flesh of her forehead. "My bounty hunter babes have been kicking ass all over the galaxy."

"Skirts?" I asked, glancing down at my battle kilt. "This is not a skirt."

Tori shrugged one shoulder, pulling a metal stick from her hair and twirling it over the tops of her fingers. "I'm not saying I don't approve. You Vandar all seem to have the legs for it."

"I did not think you noticed any legs but mine," her Dothvek mate growled, crossing the middle of the open amphitheater with a crate filled with ammunition.

Tori flashed him her pointy teeth as she smiled. "Your legs are my favorite, pretty boy."

The young Dothvek lowered his crate and gave her a reluctant smile, looping an arm around her waist and pulling her to him. "I hope so, mate."

I pulled my gaze from the pair of lovers and scanned the weapons we'd been moving from the secret armory. The bounty hunter's engineer and security chief had been inspecting everything and bringing it up to code, since the equipment had been sitting dormant for hundreds of rotations. It now appeared we had enough firepower to challenge an imperial attack, if only we had the fighters to wield them.

For not the first time since we'd started working, my gaze searched for Sienna and came up lacking. She'd slipped away sometime during the bounty hunters' arrival, and she hadn't returned. I'd been so caught up with preparing for battle and bringing the Dothveks and their females up to speed that I hadn't dwelled too much on why she'd left.

I'd have thought an entire ship filled with battle-tested warriors and bounty hunting females would have been something Sienna would relish. These females were doing what she claimed to want to do. Why would she walk away from a chance to fight by their side?

I looked up at the cave dwellings rising over the village square. She must have gone home to attend to her sister. I let my gaze fall to the rock face that held the planet's supplies. Or maybe she'd needed to attend to work. I frowned. Neither was a good enough reason for staying away when it was finally time to ready for battle. This was what I'd been preparing her for during all our training sessions.

Then I thought back to our conversation before the bounty hunter ship had arrived. The one where she'd talked to me about staying on the planet with her. Had that upset her? Was that the reason she'd run off? I grunted as I shifted one of the newly augmented launchers and tilted it to face the sky. I'd always been honest with Sienna about wanting to leave the planet and find a way back to my people.

You should have told her you want her to come with you, I scolded myself. Even though my stomach clenched at the possibility that she would say no, I needed her to know that I did not wish to leave without her.

"I need to take care of something," I told Kush, as he fitted a torpedo into its casing.

He straightened and met my eyes. "Is it about your female? The one standing with you when we arrived?"

"How did you know?"

He put a hand to his chest. "You do remember that my people are empathic?"

I hadn't, but my face warmed at the realization that he could read my thoughts.

"But even if I couldn't sense your emotions, I would know that something is amiss with a female because of the look on your face." He waved at hand at the Dothveks working in the dusty ring. "I have seen it on all my Dothvek brothers' faces at one point or another."

I rubbed a hand across the scruff of my cheeks. "It is that obvious?"

He grinned and thumped a hand on my shoulder. "It is not a bad thing to care about a female so much that it makes you sick."

I choked out a laugh. "It isn't? Doesn't it make you a more vulnerable warrior?"

Kush shook his head, his dark braid swinging. "It gives you something more powerful to fight for. Revenge is good, but love is better."

I had not expected such wisdom from the bare-chested warrior that some might consider a barbarian, but all of the Dothveks on his ship were mated to one of the bounty hunter females, and they all appeared to be just as eager for battle.

"Besides," Kush continued, giving me another thump and stepping back. "Didn't you say your female was a good fighter? We need all the warriors we can get."

"I will return," I told him, determined to find Sienna and bring her back. After I asked her to come with me when I left the planet.

I'd almost made it to the tunnel leading out of the amphitheater when a blast exploded the far end of the open air arena. My gaze snapped to the sky, where Zagrath fighters were zipping overhead, a red torrent of laser fire shooting from them. They'd arrived sooner than we'd expected.

"*Tvek!*" I yelled, looking over my shoulder at the weapons we'd assembled in the open area. The imperial attack had started before we'd had a chance to get our weapons in place or away from stray laser fire.

Holly's gold-skinned mate scooped her up and ran for the exit. "I'm getting her to safety."

I waved at the supply cave as he passed me. "Head over there. The planet's supply stores are cut into the rock. She'll be safe inside."

He nodded, not slowing his pace as the pregnant female jostled in his arms.

Instead of running, the Dothveks and Tori were busy shoving armed torpedos into launchers and swinging them toward the incoming fighters.

"Take this, you imperial fuckers!" Tori yelled, as she unleashed a torpedo into the air.

As Holly had promised, the torpedo flew with incredible speed, locking onto a gray fighter and turning it into a ball of flame.

Tori cheered at the explosion. "One down!"

Casting a lingering look at the cave dwellings and hoping Sienna was safe, I bolted back to help fire at the attackers. Vrax fed torpedos into the launcher Tori was operating, so I started doing the same for Kush.

"Thanks." He grinned as I loaded a fresh torpedo for him, then spun the launcher into the sky, tracking an imperial ship before loosing the weapon. It arched high before darting toward the fleeing ship, and soon the sky was filled with another fireball as it found its target.

A rumble made us all swivel our attention to the bounty hunter ship lifting off the ground.

"Caro can't resist a good sky battle," Tori yelled over the sound of more laser fire.

We watched as the ship shot forward, flying low and blasting a pair of imperial fighters, before flipping over and coming back around for a second run.

"She's good," I said, loading another torpedo for Kush.

"She's not just good," Tori corrected me. "She's fucking great!"

As the huge ship swooped and pivoted with the grace and agility of a much smaller ship, I had to agree with her. Two more imperial fighters blew up, but one spiraled to the ground in a fiery streak, crashing somewhere near the shallows. In the distance I heard screaming, no doubt from terrified villagers.

"Last one!" Kush said as his torpedo blew up the final gray Zagrath ship overhead.

I braced my hands on my knees to catch my breath. "Not bad for a few torpedo launchers and one ship."

Before the others could agree with me, a swarm of imperial ships descended from above, all firing on the planet and on the bounty hunter ship. Vrax pulled Tori down as laser fire blew up the benches of the amphitheater, chunks of stone raining down around us.

The bounty hunter ship flew deftly, but there were too many fighters on her tail. Like a dart, she flew away from the village in a manic, evasive pattern, disappearing entirely from our view.

"Caro!" Tori jerked from her mate's grasp and ran back to her launcher, her expression wild with rage as she aimed it at the gray ships that now filled the sky like a swarm of Zillian locusts.

When ships started to explode one after the other in quick succession, we all looked at Tori. But she hadn't fired. She gaped at the fire in the sky with as much surprise as the rest of us, as imperial fighter after imperial fighter imploded.

Then the black Vandar horde ships dropped their invisibility shielding.

CHAPTER THIRTY-FIVE

Ch 35

Corvak

I ran from the amphitheater as the Vandar transport ships descended from the larger horde ship. Most of the imperial fighters had been blasted from the sky, but a few had darted above the clouds and presumably back to the imperial battleship in orbit. Villagers who'd come from the square earlier to stare at the bounty hunter ship now took advantage of the break in laser fire to run back toward the village and the dwellings. A quick glance over my shoulder revealed a mass of bodies moving swiftly up the path.

My heart pounded as I dashed toward the trio of black ships touching down next to where the bounty hunter ship had been.

I didn't know if Raas Bron himself would be on one of the transports, but I was more than ready to bend my knee to him and show him my sincere contrition. Standing with my hands clasped behind my back and my tail only slightly twitching, I waited as patiently as I could while the ramps to the ships lowered to the hardpacked dirt.

When the Raas emerged, the metal on his studded leather arm braces glinting in the light, my mouth went dry. It was not Raas Bron, or any warlord of the Vandar I'd seen before. Since I'd laid eyes on all the current Raas' but one, this had to be Raas Vassim. The one who patrolled the far outskirts of the galaxy, and rarely had any contact with other Vandar. The one who was whispered about in low tones and with furtive glances. The one they said was deranged.

Lunori Raas, he was called in hushed tones. The Deranged Warlord.

Raiders poured from the transports behind him, but all waited with their axes and shields in their hands as the warlord took long strides toward me, his kilt slapping against his muscular thighs and his tail swishing rapidly.

"Vandar," he said, his shrewd gaze fixed on me. "It was you who called for aid?"

I clicked my heels together quickly. "It was, Raas. I am Corvak of the Vandar."

More black leather cut into the flesh of his massive chest as it crossed from the top of his shoulder to his waist. Behind him, his tail snapped back and forth as if he was an animal readying itself to pounce. "But your horde is not here."

I clenched my hands together and lifted my chin. "I am currently without a horde."

He tilted his head at me. "I'm listening."

"I was the battle chief for Raas Kratos, and then for his successor Raas Bron. When I believed the human female the Raas had claimed to be deceitful, I questioned her in my *oblek*. For that, I was exiled to this planet."

"I've heard of the Raas' and their human mates. I do not understand it." The *lunori Raas* appraised me. "I do understand wanting to punish one who is deceptive."

I inclined my head at him. He did not seem so deranged to me, but I had yet to see him in battle.

Raas Vassim flicked his gaze behind me. "Stranding you on this pre-warp planet seems like harsh punishment. Perhaps even harsher than being banished to the hinterlands of space."

I stared at him. Had the Raas been banished? I had never heard of this. Or was this a part of his madness? Was he paranoid?

"The planet of Kimithion III might be more primitive than our society, but they do not deserve to be conquered by the empire," I said, instead. "I am grateful you responded to my hails, although I am surprised you would come so far."

"Your hail was not the only one I received beckoning me to this place."

Before I could ask him who else could have possibly sent him a hail from the planet, more imperial fighters descended en masse from above. Some fired at the planet, while others targeted the main horde ship. Still other gunmetal-gray imperial transports began landing near the bank of the shallows.

Raas Vassim waved his raiders forward. My heart leapt at the sight of so many gleaming battle axes and swishing tails. I would get to fight alongside my Vandar brothers again.

"We have come to kill our enemy and aid our Vandar brother." Raas Vassim thrust his fist into the air. "For Vandar!"

I joined the other raiders in pumping my fist into the air. "For Vandar!"

The Raas cut his gaze to the imperial soldiers coming off the transports in the distance, then turned back to me. "I saw your armaments in the arena. We will handle the ground invaders. You and my horde ship can take out the vermin left in the sky."

I clicked my heels again in deference to the warlord, watching the Raas lead his raiders in an all-out run toward the advancing Zagrath. When I spun back toward the amphitheater, torpedoes were already blasting from within its confines.

I'd almost reached the entrance to the tunnel when the local fighters caught up to me. There were only a handful of the fighters that I'd trained, but they carried their makeshift shields and determined expressions.

"We're here to fight, battle chief," one of the humans yelled.

So my training hadn't been a total loss. Some of the males had courage.

"You can join us with the armaments," I said, waving for them to follow me. "I am surprised Donal and his friends are not with you. Didn't they claim to thirst for battle?"

One of the humans snorted out a laugh. "Donal's more interested in spending time with his intended than anything else."

I stopped and turned on my heel so fast the human almost smacked into me. "His intended?"

Was that why Sienna wasn't fighting by my side? Had she decided to be with Donal since I was leaving? The moment the thoughts crossed my mind, I dismissed them. Sienna detested the man. I'd seen it in her eyes every time she'd been around him. I also knew the way she looked at me. She would never betray me for that weak excuse for a male.

"The female who pretended to be one of us the first day," another fighter said. "You remember? The one you fought?"

Of course I knew he meant Sienna.

"We stopped by his dwelling so he would join us, but he said he was busy with her."

Fear iced my skin as I thought about the male Sienna had rejected time and time again. He was a coward who was not above taking something by force.

I pointed to the mouth of the tunnel. "Join the others inside. They need help loading the torpedoes."

The fighters ran forward, then the last one glanced at me over his shoulder. "What about you? Aren't you coming?"

I locked my gaze on the cave dwellings. "I have something to take care of first."

Then I ran faster than I ever had before.

CHAPTER THIRTY-SIX

Ch 36

Sienna

I glared at Donal, my head throbbing as I yanked at the bindings holding my hands together. The walls of his dwelling shook as more laser fire pounded the surface of the planet, a fine dust sifting down from the rock ceiling and dusting his brown hair as he stood across from me with his arms folded and his scowl fierce.

I'd been roused by the sounds of the low-flying ships and incoming weapons fire, and the onslaught of the attack had not faded since I'd been conscious. The empire was attacking, and I was powerless to fight. I thrashed again, almost falling off the couch. "This is crazy. You can't hold me against my will."

"It's for your own good, Sienna." His gaze shifted to the window. "It's too dangerous out there right now."

"I thought this was what you trained for," I said, attempting to appeal to his sense of male pride. "Didn't you want to be a warrior and defend the planet?"

His top lip curled. "You mean like your Vandar lover? No, let the others die in a pointless battle. When the Zagrath defeat them and take over the planet, I'll be the first to welcome them with open arms. They'll need emissaries from the community, and who better than me?"

I looked away from him, repulsed by his cowardice and disloyalty. I'd always thought he was an obnoxious jerk. How had I not seen how much worse he was?

Another blast hit the surface, and the floor trembled. Were the Zagrath firing at the cave dwellings? My gut hardened into a cold ball of fear. I did not want to end up buried beneath tons of rubble, if the tall peaks fell.

"Help!" I screamed, aiming my words at the thin curtains fluttering over the windows. "Somebody!"

My cries were drowned out by the noise of the battle and the screams of everyone else running on the path outside the dwelling, just one more voice in a chorus of terror.

Donal laughed, but it was a hard, mirthless sound. "No one is coming for you. No one knows you're here. Well, no one who would dare open their mouths about it."

I thought back to the hands grabbing me from behind. "Your friends were in on this, too?"

His cold smile was the only answer. "They don't like the idea of that barbarian showing up here and taking my girl either."

"Corvak has nothing to do with me not marrying you." I strained my hands against the rope until the skin chafed. "I was never going to marry you."

"That's where you're wrong. You are going to marry me. As soon as this is all over and the empire drags away the corpse of your Vandar, you will agree to marry me, or I'll make sure your father never works again. You really want your sweet little sister to be homeless?"

I narrowed my eyes at him. Since Juliette had been the one to tell Donal that I was seeing Corvak, and was the reason I was currently being held against my will while the planet was being brutally attacked, she was far from my favorite person at the moment. But as furious I was at her, I didn't want *that* to happen.

"You'd really force a woman to marry you?" I shook my head at him. "Why would you want someone who doesn't want you?"

His eyes flashed and he dropped his hands to his sides, clenching them into fists so hard his arms shook. "You *will* want me."

I shrank back as he stomped over to me, gripping my jaw in his hand and jerking my face to his. "Once that Vandar is gone, you'll forget all about him, and I'll *make* you want me."

I twisted my face from his painful grasp. Even though Donal looked a little crazy, I refused to let him scare me. A Vandar warrior would never back down from a fight, and neither would I. "That's not the way it works, Donal. I'm in love with Corvak, and I always will be." A blast rattled the door and sent more dust over us. "It doesn't matter if he dies or if he leaves, I'll never stop loving him. And I'll never love you."

He staggered back like he'd been slapped, shaking his head so hard it was a blur. I used his distraction to pull my shoulders back as far as I could and tug my hands with all my might. The pain made me flinch as I scraped off the skin on my wrists, but one hand finally slipped free. I let out a gasp, drawing Donal's attention.

"What are you…" His words died on his lips as his gaze dropped to my neck. Then he was on me, tearing back the neckline of my blouse. "What is this? Where did you get this?"

I didn't know what he was talking about, but he was so distracted pawing at my collarbone that I was able to use my free hand to untie my other one. When both hands were free from the restraints, I brought them around and down hard on his back.

A huff of startled breath escaped his lips as he rolled off me and onto the floor. Leaping up, I kicked him in the gut, rewarded by a groan as he clutched his belly. "That's for trying to rape me." I aimed another kick at his side. "That's for tying me up." My final kick was straight at his groin. "And that's for never ever learning the meaning of the word no, you spoiled, little prick."

Stepping over the moaning man, I glanced down at my wrists. They were a bloody mess, but I didn't care. I was getting the hell away and joining the fight. Bandages could wait for later.

I pushed open the door and ran out onto the path. Villagers were rushing in both directions, the din of yelling and crying almost drowning out the sound of fighters swarming overhead. The sky glowed with the red beams of laser fire and the orange bursts of explosions.

I turned to rush down toward the village square and ran smack into a sweaty, bare chest. My fingers splayed across the hard muscles as I braced myself and peered up at the face of the Vandar raider.

"Sienna!" Corvak closed his hands over mine, his gaze raking across my face. "I thought you were…"

"I was detained," I said. "I see you started the war without me."

Corvak cocked one eyebrow, squeezing my hands to his hot flesh. When I flinched from the contact on my raw wrists, his gaze dropped to them. Then his face became stone.

"What happened?" He gently lifted my hands, a muscle ticking in his clenched jaw. "Who did this to you?"

"Don't worry about him. He's currently searching for his balls."

The fury faded from his face. "That's the warrior I trained."

A few villagers bumped into us, and Corvak pulled us over to the side so the crowd could pass.

"Shouldn't you get back to the fighting?" I asked. "I'm ready to fight with you."

"Not until you know that I'm not leaving this planet without you."

I held my breath for a beat. "What do you mean? You want to stay?"

He lifted one of my palms and pressed a kiss to it. "I want you to come with me. After we defeat the empire and secure the future of the planet, I'll be leaving with the bounty hunters. They've offered me a place on their crew. I want you to join me."

My pulse fluttered. "Live on a bounty hunter spaceship?"

"You'd get to do what you love to do, and you'd do it by my side." He traced a finger along the line of my jaw and down my neck, hesitating when his callused finger reached the hollow of my throat. His dark eyes flashed with possessive desire. "As my mate."

I tried to swallow, but my throat was too thick. Instead, my mouth fell open.

Corvak dragged his hand down, pulling the fabric of my shirt aside like Donal had done, but more gently, his fingers caressing the burning flesh that prickled from his touch. "You have my mating marks."

I instinctively attempted to look down at my own neck, but it was impossible.

"Are my marks expanding?" he asked, touching a hand to his own chest.

I glanced at the black swirls adorning his chest that I knew so well, my breath hitching when I realized that they were different. "They've spread up your neck and down your shoulders."

A deep growl escaped his lips. "This means we are true mates."

"I don't understand." How could I get Vandar marks? "I'm not a Vandar."

A smile teased his mouth. "Human females can get our marks. A Vandar only has one true mate, and when we find that mate, our marks will grow and appear on our mate's flesh as well. It also means that now our mating can produce a child."

Primal arousal pulsed through me at the thought of being marked by Corvak. "This means…?"

"What I have known in my heart for a while, Sienna," he husked. "You are the only female for me. You are mine and will always be mine. Will you come with me and be my warrior mate?"

I was overwhelmed with emotions, but the answer was so easy it tripped off my lips. "Yes, of course. I've always been yours."

When his mouth crashed into mine, and he swept me into a wild embrace, all rational thought left my mind. I didn't even notice when the imperial battleship exploded and turned the sky white or when all the fighters were then picked from the sky one by one. Only when the blasts stopped, and the skies went quiet did Corvak and I rip ourselves apart from each other.

CHAPTER THIRTY-SEVEN

Ch 37

Corvak

"You are sure?" Raas Vassim eyed me, his thick arms crossed over his chest. The suns were setting, sending warm light shooting across the shallows and backlighting the fierce warlord. The effect was that the Raas appeared before me almost in shadow, masking the blood smeared across his chest, and even his face. I hadn't seen the remains of the imperial soldiers who'd been unfortunate enough to land on the planet, but there were whispers that their bodies were hacked to bits.

I clicked my heels and bowed my head. "I am grateful for the offer, Raas, but I promised my mate that we would stay closer to Kimithion III."

He grunted, making it clear what he thought of my answer, but he nodded. "I do not understand the appeal of these human females, but I respect your mating marks. If you have made a promise, you should keep it. It is true we will be returning to the hinterlands once we leave this primitive place."

He glanced back at his raiders who were preparing their transports for departure, although the ship that the Raas stood in front of was larger than a usual transport. I'd noticed that all of Raas Vassim's ships were augmented to look even more terrifying than our warbirds, with spikes bolted to the metal hulls. I suspected it took an even firmer hand to rule a sector that was defined by its lawlessness and brutality.

"The residents of Kimithion III extend their gratitude for your assistance, as do I. We would not have defeated the empire without you and your raiders."

"That is true." He unfolded his arms and rested one hand on the hilt of his battle axe, drumming his fingers. "Destroying a Zagrath battleship was its own reward, as was cutting down the soldiers they sent to the surface. It has been too long since my warriors and I tasted imperial blood."

I forced myself not to look at the flecks of blood on his cheek. Were the rumors true? Did the *Lunori Raas* tear into his enemy with his teeth?

As if reading my mind, the edges of his mouth quivered. "If you ever tire of hunting bounties, you always have a place in my horde. Your lust for vengeance and talent for torture would be put to good use, battle chief."

"It would be an honor to serve you, Raas."

His gaze flicked over my shoulder. "Once you have sated your lust for your mate, of course. There is no place for a female on a Vandar warbird roaming the hinterlands, even one who fights."

"Yes, Raas." I did not need to turn to know that Sienna was approaching. I could sense the change in the air and the tingle skating across my skin.

Raas Vassim turned to board his transport then pivoted back around. "One more thing, Corvak. The empire sent a lot of firepower to take a planet of caves and dirt. I suspect it does not have anything to do with their plentiful algae."

"It does not," I admitted. The information about Kimithion III was so sensitive I hesitated to share it, even with one who'd been responsible for saving the planet from the Zagrath.

He raised a palm. "You do not need to tell me. It is better I do not know. That way, I do not have to deny anything." He twisted the hand to reveal a thin scar across the back of it. "I suspect it has something to do with my vanishing scar."

I opened my mouth, but he shook his head. "Do not worry, battle chief. Their secret is safe with me. The last thing I would wish for is immortality or regeneration. Not when I chase death with such determination."

I didn't know how to respond to that, so I didn't, clamping my mouth shut and giving him a single nod.

The Raas turned and joined his warriors who were debating over the wooden boxes of algae tea and kelp jerky that the Kimitherians had insisted on gifting them after the battle.

"Did he take it well?" Sienna slipped her hand in mine as she joined me.

"Me not joining the horde?" I threaded my fingers through hers and walked her away from the Vandar ships and toward the hulking bounty hunter cruiser. "He understood."

"I'm surprised. He doesn't strike me as a true love kind of guy."

I stole a quick glance back at the Raas they said was deranged. He didn't look much different from the Raas' I knew, although I'd recognized a fury behind his eyes that he might not always be able to control. "He respects our mating marks. They are Vandar tradition."

Sienna brushed her fingertips across the dark swirls that had appeared on her chest. "Even though I've seen them with my own eyes, it's hard to believe it. These things don't come off."

I tilted my head at her. "You wish them to come off?"

"I didn't say that, but being marked takes a little getting used to."

I wrapped an arm around her waist. "I never imagined I would see my mating marks on a human female, but now I cannot imagine them on anyone else."

"At least I don't have to worry about telling everyone we're together. The marks do the trick pretty well."

A possessive growl rumbled deep in my throat. "They tell the universe that you are mine. What did your sister say when she saw them?"

Sienna's mouth thinned into a tight line. She'd returned to her quarters to pack her meager belongings before our departure and to say her goodbyes. "I didn't see Juliette or my father. He's probably drinking with his buddies to celebrate a victory they had no part in, and I don't know where my sister is. Too afraid to show her face after she betrayed me?"

As a Vandar, I'd been trained to have very little tolerance for duplicity and disloyalty. But I also knew how much Sienna's younger sister meant to her. "She could not have known what Donal would do with the information she gave him."

Sienna pulled back and looked askance at me. "Don't tell me you're taking her side? Because of her, I was knocked out and tied up. Who knows what that asshole would have done to me if I hadn't gotten away from him? Even if she didn't know he would go that far, she still shouldn't have picked him over me." Her voice cracked. "I'm her sister, and she betrayed me."

"You will not see her before we leave? Although we will not fly as far as the hinterlands, I cannot guarantee where the bounties will take us. It could be a while before we pass by Kimithion III again."

"Then she'll have time to think about how much she hurt me," Sienna snapped. "I left her a note telling her that I'm leaving with you and why, but I just can't see her right now." She touched a hand to her bandaged wrists. "I'm afraid I'll say something I'll regret."

"Something you will regret more than leaving her without saying goodbye?"

"Yes." She shifted her gaze to the cave dwellings that were being bathed in the golden light of the setting suns. "In my note, I told her I would come back for her one day, and maybe then she'd be ready to leave. I know she isn't now. She doesn't have the courage, and I can't give it to her."

I peered over my shoulder, hoping to see the curvy blonde running toward us. But there was nothing but the Vandar packing up to leave, and some stragglers from the village watching the rare sight of alien ships departing from their planet.

"At least we're leaving the planet with improved defenses and updated communications systems. If the Zagrath so much as glance at Kimithion III, messages will go out on all encrypted frequencies."

Sienna let out a relieved sigh. "And maybe all the Zagrath who knew about the planet's unusual properties were eliminated in the attack. The Vandar and bounty hunters did take out a sizable battleship and at least a hundred fighters."

I made a mental calculation of all the Zagrath battleships the Vandar had destroyed recently. Entire fleets had been taken out when the hordes had worked together, and now we could add another significant blow against the empire's might. After making small dents in the enemy's formidable armor for a long time, the momentum finally seemed to be in favor of the resistance.

I took Sienna's hand in mine and led her to the ramp of the bounty hunter ship. "Then you're ready to join your new crew?"

She pivoted toward the village one last time, her gaze lingering on the place she'd lived for all her life. I wondered how many good memories were mixed in with the bad.

When she turned back to me, her eyes glistened. "I'm ready."

Tori poked her head from the ship. "Skirts here says you're a decent fighter. You interested in joining the security team?"

Sienna's face lit up. "Do you get to kick ass?"

Tori flashed her a pointy grin. "Hell yeah, we do." She waved us on board. Come on up. Caro's itching to take off."

We walked up the steel ramp as the engines fired up. Footsteps echoed as crew members bustled around, preparing for the imminent departure. Kush met us at the top, clasping my arm with his hand as the ramp slammed shut behind us.

"Welcome to the crew!" Holly called out from one of the corridors that split off the central belly of the vessel.

A small ball of green fur rolled by us, making what sounded like barking noises followed by a loud purr.

"We are more than a crew," Kush said, squeezing my arm. "Welcome to the family."

I cut my eyes to Sienna, who was beaming. I was back on a ship with brave warriors, and now I had my mate by my side. It was good to be part of a family again.

EPILOGUE

Juliette

I hurried across the village square, hoping the darkness would mask me. The strap of my bag dug into my shoulder and I hitched it higher, wishing I hadn't decided to bring so much with me. Then again, I was leaving for good.

Casting a quick glance back at the stone obelisk in the center of the square, I swallowed down any remnants of hesitation and fear. I couldn't be afraid, if I was going to stow away on the alien ship with my sister. Even though Sienna was still furious at me, she'd have to forgive me once she realized we were stuck together in space. Of course, I'd have to hide on the ship until we were well away from Kimithion III. If my sister caught me before then, she might send me right back.

I clenched my jaw, determination urging me forward. I was not going to be left behind. Now that Sienna was leaving with Corvak, there was nothing left for me on the planet. Just days stretching out endlessly, worrying about my drunk father. Even marriage wouldn't take me away from his shadow, not that anyone would want me now that I was the sister of the woman who'd taken a barbarian as a mate. Kimithion III was a lot of things, but forgiving wasn't one of them, and people who were immortal had very long memories.

The three moons that usually glowed in the sky were all dim tonight, so the path was darker than usual as I hurried past the amphitheater and toward the hulking ship firing up for departure. One of the ships who'd come to the aid of the planet had already departed, but word had reached me that the ship Sienna was leaving on with her Vandar had not.

I hadn't gotten much of a look at the bounty hunter ship when it had landed, but it looked even more menacing now with its dark outspread wings that curved toward the ground. Nerves made my stomach do a flip as I peered up at the looming ship, more beast than bird. Could I really do this? Could I actually stowaway with the Dothveks and female bounty hunters and spend the rest of my life with them?

I hesitated at the base of the ramp, glowing blue lights in the metal floor providing the only illumination into the pitch blackness of the ship. From what I'd seen of the bounty hunters, they were impressive. Even the pregnant females had taken part in preparing the planet for the attack. Brave women like that wouldn't be so bad to live with.

I tightened my grip around the strap of my bag and rushed up the sloped steel and into the ship before I could talk myself out of it. Once I was inside, I blew out a breath as my heart hammered in my chest. This was by far the most daring thing I'd ever done, and I just hoped I would be able to get through it without puking.

As my eyes adjusted to the blackness, I glanced around furtively. The engines rumbled loudly now, and a deep voice bellowed from the front of the ship. I ducked down a short corridor, a little surprised that the ship all the bounty hunters lived on wasn't bigger inside. When footsteps thundered toward me, I slipped through a door and into what appeared to be a cramped storage closet.

Okay, not the greatest place to stow away, but not the worst. At least I couldn't be seen. The rumbling of the engine was now a roar, and my stomach lurched when the ship lifted off the ground. It took every ounce of self-control—and fingernails digging into my arm—not to rush out and beg to be returned to my home world. But when I imagined my sister's face as I begged to go home, I knew I'd never do it. She already thought I was a traitor. I wasn't going to let her think I was also a coward.

"No turning back now," I whispered to myself, my soft voice a comfort in the darkness.

I focused on my breathing as I stood in the dark closet, waiting to be far enough away that I could reveal myself. I wasn't sure how long that would be, but when the ship jolted and the engines powered down, I nervously nibbled my thumbnail.

Had we returned to the planet for some reason? Was there any way they could know I was here?

Voices boomed around me, and then grew fainter. What was going on? The ship was no longer flying, and it sounded like the crew was disembarking. I opened the door and peeked out. The ramp was down again but instead of darkness outside, light poured in.

I tiptoed to the top of the ramp, peering down. Instead of dirt, the ramp rested on a shiny floor. Where was I? It wasn't Kimithion III, that was certain.

I walked down slowly, bending my head and gasping when I realized I was inside another, much larger, ship. At the bottom of the ramp, staring up at me with equal shock were a cluster of bare-chested Vandar raiders.

The hammering of my heart was almost deafening as the warrior in the center stepped forward, his tail snapping behind him. Black studded leather sheathed his forearms, and a matching strap crossed his chest, spiked armor extending over one shoulder. Straight hair as black as ink fell down his back and the dark slashes of his eyebrows pressed together.

"Who are you?" I asked, hearing the traitorous shake in my voice.

He cocked his head slightly at me, his tail curving up behind his back and going still, only the tip quivering. "I am Raas Vassim of the Vandar, but many call me *Lunori Raas*, the Deranged Warlord."

I met his gaze, the dark, cunning eyes of the predator shifting down my body and the pupils widening with something I'd never seen directed my way before—raw desire. Then my eyes fluttered closed, and I fainted to the floor.

Thank you for reading PUNISHED! If you liked this alien barbarian romance, you'll love PROVOKED, book 6 in the series featuring Juliette and Raas Vassim.

I snuck onto the wrong ship. Now I'm at the mercy of the most terrifying and deadly of the Vandar warlords—and he refuses to let me go.

One-click PROVOKED Now>

Want a BONUS EPILOGUE featuring the three Vandar warlord brothers and their human mates? Join my VIP Reader group and get PILLAGED AGAIN to see what happens after the welcome home banquet in book 3!

https://BookHip.com/DWLCX

ALSO BY TANA STONE

Raider Warlords of the Vandar Series:

POSSESSED (also available in AUDIO)

PLUNDERED (also available in AUDIO)

PILLAGED

PURSUED

PUNISHED

PROVOKED

Alien Academy Series:

ROGUE (also available in AUDIO)

The Tribute Brides of the Drexian Warriors Series:

TAMED (also available in AUDIO)

SEIZED (also available in AUDIO)

EXPOSED (also available in AUDIO)

RANSOMED (also available in AUDIO)

FORBIDDEN (also available in AUDIO)

BOUND (also available in AUDIO)

JINGLED (A Holiday Novella)

CRAVED (also available in AUDIO)

STOLEN

SCARRED

The Barbarians of the Sand Planet Series:

BOUNTY (also available in AUDIO)

CAPTIVE (also available in AUDIO)

TORMENT (also available on AUDIO)

TRIBUTE (also available as AUDIO)

SAVAGE

CLAIM

TANA STONE books available as audiobooks!

RAIDER WARLORDS OF THE VANDAR:

POSSESSED on AUDIBLE

PLUNDERED on AUDIBLE

Alien Academy Series:

ROGUE on AUDIBLE

BARBARIANS OF THE SAND PLANET

BOUNTY on AUDIBLE

CAPTIVE on AUDIBLE

TORMENT on AUDIBLE

TRIBUTE on AUDIBLE

TRIBUTE BRIDES OF THE DREXIAN WARRIORS

TAMED on AUDIBLE

SEIZED on AUDIBLE

EXPOSED on AUDIBLE

RANSOMED on AUDIBLE

FORBIDDEN on AUDIBLE

BOUND on AUDIBLE

CRAVED on AUDIBLE

ABOUT THE AUTHOR

Tana Stone is a bestselling sci-fi romance author who loves sexy aliens and independent heroines. Her favorite superhero is Thor (with Aquaman a close second because, well, Jason Momoa), her favorite dessert is key lime pie (okay, fine, *all* pie), and she loves Star Wars and Star Trek equally. She still laments the loss of *Firefly*.

She has one husband, two teenagers, and two neurotic cats. She sometimes wishes she could teleport to a holographic space station like the one in her tribute brides series (or maybe vacation at the oasis with the sand planet barbarians). :-)

She loves hearing from readers! Email her any questions or comments at tana@tanastone.com.

Want to hang out with Tana in her private Facebook group? Join on all the fun at: https://www.facebook.com/groups/tanastonestributes/

Copyright © 2021 by Broadmoor Books

Cover Design by Croco Designs

Editing by Tanya Saari

All rights reserved.

No part of this book may be reproduced in any form or by any electronic or mechanical means, including information storage and retrieval systems, without written permission from the author, except for the use of brief quotations in a book review.

This is a work of fiction. Names, characters, places, and incidents are the products of the author's imagination or are used fictitiously and are not to be construed as real. Any resemblance to actual events, locales, organizations, or persons, living or dead, is entirely coincidental.

Printed in Great Britain
by Amazon